D1534285

THE FIRE OF LOVE

JOSÉ LUIS OLAIZOLA

THE FIRE OF LOVE

A Historical Novel about Saint John of the Cross

TRANSLATED BY STEPHEN CARO

IGNATIUS PRESS   SAN FRANCISCO

Original Spanish edition:
Los amores de san Juan de la Cruz
© 1999 Ediciones Martínez Roca, S.A., Barcelona

Cover art from Restored Traditions

Cover design by Riz Boncan Marsella

Contents

Chapter 1

From Silk to Swine

Gonzalo de Yepes, a handsome, high-spirited young man, is believed to have been born in the Castilian village of Tordesillas in 1508. The son of a wealthy landowner, he was educated by a priest in Bercero, and did so well at his books that his father decided to send him to the University of Salamanca.

This did not please his mother. She was of the opinion that he had already received more than enough education. What did a *caballero*, a gentleman, need with an education? His duty, she felt, was to find a fitting wife for the Yepes dynasty. The Yepeses were an illustrious family of silk merchants in Castile, León and Asturias and their line could be traced back several generations.

The Yepeses lived in Castile's principal center of commerce, Medina del Campo, whose fairs and markets drew wealthy merchants from as far afield as the Low Countries. Although for the most part only distantly related, the Yepeses treated each other like siblings. There had been a standing agreement since 1480 that a member of the family would act as *paterfamilias* and be responsible for the settling of all disputes concerning the business, or any other family matter, without rancor or recourse to the law.

At the family meeting of 1480, Don Juan de Yepes, precentor of the Burgos Cathedral, was nominated as head of the family. On his wife's death he was ordained a priest and appears to have carried out his sacred ministry without blemish. Like all the Yepeses, he had traveled widely throughout Europe in his youth as a silk merchant. And to the worldly wisdom he acquired in this trade he added the qualities conferred by holy orders, studiousness and austerity. It seems, moreover, that he never lost the soundness of judgment needed for the important business of advising the family. He was said to be the best-dressed cleric in Castile, his many cassocks and capes always being of the finest silk. He was a Yepes after all and, without wishing to cut too fine a figure, must dress like one.

The Yepeses, one and all, seem to have been driven by a single aim—the acquisition of land. No matter how much or how little they could afford, whether it was to be put to the plow, cultivated or left as woodland for hunting deer, quail and pigeon in early autumn, buying land was the thing. The family also owned extensive tracts of grazing land for cattle, sheep and goats. With the approach of winter, their herds were driven to the pastures of Extremadura and Andalusia. This obsession for land stemmed from the knowledge that profitable as the silk trade was, it was a risky business. Many of their supply routes passed through Italy and Crete and were constantly under threat from "the Turk".

The Yepeses also put their charitable works onto a formal footing. In line with common religious observance, a tenth of the family's income was given away. This was mostly left up to Canon Don Juan. He warned the family to be scrupulous about charity and not try to fix the books. They might pull the wool over his eyes, but they could not deceive God. And he would quote the story of Ananias and his wife, who were struck down at the feet of Saint Peter for pocketing part of the proceeds from the sale of a field. There was a good deal of discussion among the Yepeses about what constituted a tenth, but the canon's warnings were generally heeded. He was even more severe about greed than lust, giving them chapter and verse from both Old Testament and New to prove that God was less tolerant of avarice than of sins of the flesh. Not all the Yepeses were as irreproachable as the canon. Most notable among a string of scandalous cases was that of García Menendez de Yepes, who turned out to have a second family in Lyons, a city which has been famous for its silkworms since Roman times and to which he traveled regularly to buy silk.

This kind of thing occurred so frequently among the nobility and even the royal family, however, that Don Juan barely raised an eyebrow when he heard of it. He urged them to espouse marital fidelity and guard against temptation on their journeys. He recommended them to avoid inns wherever possible and to stay at monasteries or in the homes of honest people who had been vouched for by the Church. And in a tone of dire admonition he would add that he knew what he was talking about. He had chosen the path of righteousness at an early age, for he knew how easily the devil could make that path his own, placing temptation in the way of good Christians where they are most vulnerable.

When Gonzalo's father, Don Gonzalo, turned forty, he did something that sent a shock wave through the Yepes clan. He bought a farm on the banks of the Tagus outside the small town of Yepes near Toledo, where the family had originated. After many years in the silk trade, he felt he had earned the right to retire. The family were dismayed. What if others were to follow suit? Would it not undermine their position in the marketplace, which was built on a system of quid pro quo? Moreover, would it not allow "outsiders" to gain a foothold in a business that had been in the family for generations?

This was a thinly veiled reference to the Jews, who dominated the silk trade in France and Italy and had their eye on Castile. Indeed, the whole of Europe had been casting a covetous eye on Spain since the moment when wealth began to pour in from the New World, especially the gold and silver now flowing into the country in quantities that were beyond imagination. And it had not escaped the Jews that such fabulous wealth in the form of silk might give the lie to the saying that "an ape in rich attire is still an ape." Suffering persecution since the Crucifixion, the Jews saw wealth as the best means of mitigating the blame directed toward them. They used their wealth to gain influence with those in positions of power, such as Charles V, who attained the German throne with the help of Jewish money.

But their money was also their undoing, condemned as they all too often were to exile, and their wealth confiscated. The Yepeses were not exempt from anti-Semitic feelings, there being no greater bigot than one who despises his own kind. For although they passed themselves off as *cristianos viejos*, old Christians, the first Yepes to go into the silk trade was a Jew from the Toledo synagogue.

Don Gonzalo's decision to retire to the country was widely condemned by the Yepeses. Not so by Canon Don Juan, however. The head of the family even praised Don Gonzalo's judgment, saying that an excessive desire for material possessions was injurious to the soul. Indeed, the canon had half a mind to give up his canonry and go into a Carthusian monastery to make the most of what time he had left. In the event, it was somewhat shorter than he had bargained for. Not long after this he died of dropsy, a common illness at that time.

The position of "head of the family" went to the man who had been most successful in the family business. Not content merely to buy and sell silk, he had gone into manufacturing. He had a number of large workshops built and imported looms from Antwerp. He began by producing fine cloaks for the gentry and another line of coarser stuff for military uniforms. It was with these that he made his fortune, building up such good relationships with the quartermasters of the king's army that it would have been a job to find a single soldier in the region of Medina, Valladolid and Burgos who was not wearing one of his cloaks.

His name was Hernando Aguilera de Yepes. The younger members of the family looked up to him as an example of how to get on in the trade. Few questioned his right to settle any dispute between them. His first act was to announce that since charity in the true sense of the word begins at home, the controversial question of "the tenth" would only apply once all present and future needs of the family had been attended to. He ordered the building of a large granary, which was to be kept full to the rafters against years of drought and poor harvests. He also used the money from "the tenth" to buy a valley on a tributary of the Duero known as the Cantarranas. It was excellent grazing land, and he stocked it with cattle from the Guipúzcoa region. (These were superior to Castilian cattle.) On Saint Anthony's Day he would have all the calves blessed, and he took their excellent condition as a sign of God's favor, happy in the knowledge that the Yepeses, hard workers and caring neighbors one and all, would never starve.

Whether the late canon would have approved is doubtful. He would probably have pointed out the story of the rich man who built some barns following a good harvest and went to bed, his conscience easy, only to die that very night. But Don Hernando also knew how to interpret the Scriptures without completely disregarding charity. In years of plenty he would allow a tenth of the harvest to be taken from the collective granary and distributed among the poor. This did not sit well with the consciences of some of the Yepeses, who knew very well that they were sharing out a tenth of a tenth. But they bowed to the authority of their chosen patriarch. As for the stock, in good years he would give the oldest cows to the poor.

Under Don Hernando the many branches of the Yepes family prospered. He gave them the benefit of his considerable experience, instructing them in the art of weaving, and keeping the government officials happy in order to secure their orders for cloth. At the same time he turned a blind eye to his family members' faults and misdemeanors, so long as they did not bring dishonor on the family. To keep one's word and not to lie: as far as he was concerned, little else mattered much. And he compared himself and the family to a kingdom whose wayward subjects prospered under the rule of a benevolent despot.

Don Hernando believed that the valley with its fine barn and livestock would bind the family together. Every spring, at his insistence, the whole clan got together for a feast of roast oxen and veal. Not only were the servants and their families invited but also the paupers, although these were kept at a distance. Some years there were more than two hundred guests, and no one went away hungry. Occasionally one of the many priests at the feast would make pointed remarks about Don Hernando's somewhat loose interpretation of the tenth he owed the Church. But he knew how to deal with these, too, lavishing special attentions on them.

Don Gonzalo had almost succeeded in slipping into the oblivion he sought when a piece of extraordinary news reached Medina. The family had understood him to have turned his back on business affairs to live out his days by the banks of the Tagus and give himself wholly to bringing up his only son. Then it emerged he had embarked on a disastrous pig-keeping venture.

"Pigs!" Don Hernando exclaimed. "A Yepes keeping pigs? What next?"

He immediately dispatched a servant to Toledo to find out exactly what was going on. The servant, Tomás by name, sent the following report to Don Hernando.

I found the farm in a state of neglect, the fields gone to seed and Don Gonzalo at death's door. He was attended only by an old woman servant and by his son Gonzalo, who was kneeling by his bedside. With tears in his eyes the young man begged his father not to lament the loss of his fortune, for he had two strong arms with which he would provide for them both. Don Gonzalo marveled at his son's goodness, saying he was the only comfort left to him in his misfortune.

It took me some time to learn the truth, for Don Gonzalo was on his deathbed, and between fits of raving and bouts of weeping, he would lapse into unconsciousness or fall asleep. Often we thought he had expired. Then he would wake with a start and begin to weep again and castigate himself and bemoan his ruin. But at last, with help from his son and the old woman servant, I was able to piece together the story, which to the best of my knowledge is as follows:

It seems Don Gonzalo fell in with a cousin of his wife's, a Toledan with important connections. The fellow told Don Gonzalo that for a man of his age and a man of the world, he had afforded himself a little too much ease in his retirement. In short, he was squandering his talents. Since he had nothing to do but watch his wheat grow, the fellow went on, was it not his duty to remember that he had a son in the flower of his youth with good prospects? Did not the boy deserve better than to while away his days writing verses by the riverside? Don Gonzalo replied that he intended to send him to Salamanca, whereupon the man exclaimed that Salamanca had ruined many such young men.

"Do you want him to end up in a monastery?" the fellow said. "What's in Salamanca that cannot be found in Toledo, not a stone's throw from here?"

And he assured Don Gonzalo that in Toledo he would find what he would not in Salamanca, a thing such as befitted his lineage, namely, a young lady from the Toledan nobility to marry. And if the boy was as nimble-witted as his father claimed, what was to stop him from rising to the position of mayor, or secretary of some eminent courtier, or, why not, even from becoming the emperor himself, for his connections were such that he could help the boy on his way.

With a mother's eye, Don Gonzalo's wife, who is not only younger but shrewder and, I believe, a good deal more ambitious than he, saw a chance for her son to better himself under her relative's wing.

The Toledan persuaded Don Gonzalo to make some improvements to the farm. The bigger and finer it was, the better the match his son would make. It is here that the trouble really began, for it seems the fellow suggested buying some pigs and exporting them to the island of Hispaniola, where pigs are paid for in gold.

"Pigs?! A Yepes a pig farmer?!" Don Gonzalo exclaimed, a sentiment that I warrant Your Honor would echo.

"Why not?" the fellow continued. "Surely you do not consider the pig to be unclean, as do the Jews?"

Though Tomás does not comment on this, the remark must have hit home. The pig was the subject of considerable controversy at the time. Shunned by both Jews and Muslims for religious reasons, it was highly prized in the recently discovered New World. Its superb adaptability in the Caribbean ensured that no ship set sail for the Indies without a cargo of pigs, whether in the form of livestock or salt pork. As a result, many well-to-do yeoman farmers took up pig farming, and even the president of the Council of the Indies exported a herd of pigs to the settlers of Hispaniola [the Dominican Republic] and Cuba. He is said to have made more money from the pig trade than from the slave trade. Pigs were not only stronger and faster-growing than slaves, they did not die in such appalling numbers on the journey.

The servant Tomás continues:

> Whether to placate his wife, or to avoid being thought proud, Don Gonzalo agreed to get into the export of pigs to the Indies. The Toledan would buy the pigs and take them to Seville, where he would find a ship to transport them.

Either the Toledan's name is unknown or Don Gonzalo chose not to name him on his deathbed, not wishing perhaps to take bitterness with him beyond the grave. The servant, Tomás, refers to him simply as "the Toledan". The fate of Don Gonzalo's wife is also unknown. She may well have gone mad, or died of vexation when they were ruined. We do, however, know that young Gonzalo was not involved in the venture. In an attempt to turn him into a gentleman, he was sent to the house of a nobleman in Toledo who, despite having fallen on hard times, still had access to the inner circles at court, which was then in Toledo. What Gonzalo gained from the experience is also unclear. But he never forgave himself for his failure to resist "the allure of the Sirens' song", as he was to describe it. If he had stayed by his father's side, it would have been a different song, for two heads were better than one.

The direst of predictions was now borne out by events. Leaving aside the money that the Toledan pocketed, a plague of giant bluebottle flies produced an outbreak of swine-fever. There was little that could be done about this except to track down and cull every infected animal. This was in fact precisely what the authorities ordered at the time Don Gonzalo's herd of pigs was on the so-called pork trail. This woodland trail, running from Trujillo to Seville, was guarded by the rural watch, who protected the drovers and their herds from cattle thieves.

In this instance the watch had orders to ensure that every pig with any sign of swine-fever be culled and buried in quicklime-filled trenches by the side of the trail. This was the first mishap to befall the ill-fated pig-keeping venture. Few herds were so decimated by this cull as Don Gonzalo's, and there is no record of a single pig belonging to him reaching Seville safely.

Tomás' account continues:

From Seville, which as Your Honor well knows, is the hub of the trade with the Indies, the Toledan wrote to Don Gonzalo urging him not merely to recover his losses but to make a real profit. For as a consequence of this catastrophe, the price of pigs would go through the roof. Pigs would now be worth their weight in gold. He claimed to have found some grazing land untouched by disease, high up on the slopes of the Sierra Madroñera, where the air was very pure. If ever there was a time to buy land it was now, as much as he could. And he urged the renting of as much again. By the time the year was out, he assured Don Gonzalo, they would all be rich.

Having used much of his savings in the first instance, Don Gonzalo now did something that I cannot for the life of me understand. He gave the Toledan the power to raise a loan on the security of this estate, thus ensuring his total ruin. As Your Honor knows, the Yepes family are in the habit of lending each other money free of interest. Loans are never solicited from outsiders, least of all Jews and usurers. This is such an inexorable rule that it is beyond me how a man with so much experience in the world of commerce could have committed such folly. The Sierra Madroñera herds have not been heard of again. As for the Toledan, there has been nothing but news of one calamity after another that I cannot but attribute to a fate so ruinous that it seems it even sank a ship that was about to set sail with a cargo of pigs as it rode at anchor off Sanlúcar de Barrameda.

The Toledan has not dared to show his face on this estate to give an account of his management of Don Gonzalo's affairs. Nor, I warrant, will he do so. Not so the bailiffs, however, who came not long since with a fistful of writs and injunctions conveying the somber threat of debtor's prison if, as the law demands, the value of the goods and chattels seized is insufficient to cover the debt.

Don Gonzalo declared that he would sooner die. Having been an honorable merchant all his life, he considered debtor's prison to be a fate worse than the gallows.

From that day, he gave himself up for dead. He did not have long to wait, for he died after only three days. Turning a deaf ear to all his son's attempts to console him with words of encouragement and assurances that with his shoulder to the wheel they would pull through, he died like a good Christian, in a state of deep contrition, ceaselessly urging his son not to follow in his footsteps. I believe, though I say so myself, that he also derived some comfort from my presence. As an old and, I hope, trusted servant of this family, which I have had the honor to serve all my life, Don Gonzalo confided in me. He begged me to take his son back to Medina, for he has had no part in his father's folly and bears a name that does not merit such calamity as befell him. This I gave him my word to do. And, once I have attended to the remaining business touching the estate, I propose to bring him with me when I set out on my return to Medina, and beg Your Honor to confirm that this meets with your wishes. He also asked me to say with what deep compunction he regretted having cut himself off from the rest of the family. And he asked me to tell Your Honor that if the venture had been to do with silk, a business about which he knew a thing or two, it would have turned out very differently.

When Don Hernando received Tomás' letter, he made a show of grief at the death of his relative. In fact, he could not have been more delighted. It gave him an opportunity to remind the family of the fate awaiting the sheep that strays from the fold. And he quoted the parable of the prodigal son, casting himself as the loving father who greeted his wayward son with open arms.

Chapter 2

The Splendor of the Yepeses

Don Hernando Aguilera de Yepes was then in his early forties. His four daughters, despite having few accomplishments, all had dowries and were consequently much sought after in marriage. What he lacked was a male heir. He was even said to have resorted to an infamous *curandera*, or folk healer, in an attempt to procure one. But to his undying shame this had not succeeded. As a result he was very preoccupied about his prospective sons-in-law, as they would have to replace the sons whom God in His wisdom had seen fit to deny him.

When he heard of Don Gonzalo's death, he sent enough money to ensure a decent funeral. It would not have done for a Yepes to be buried in a pauper's grave. Observing the forms that governed the paying of respects, he received Don Gonzalo's son with open arms, then sent him to live on a small farm on the outskirts of Medina. He soon discovered, however, that Gonzalo was far better educated than most of his employees and brought him to live in his own house, an imposing mansion on Medina's main street, large enough to house a dozen or more servants in the basement.

He also had an African slave. This slave was tolerably well treated and had even been allowed to marry a mulatto woman who had come from Portugal. It was not uncommon to find slaves working as liveried coachmen or grooms in Andalusia and Portugal. There was no such custom in Castile, however, and many a disapproving eyebrow had been raised at it. But Don Hernando felt that it elevated the status of the household. That they were little more than human baggage, deprived of liberty and rights, and paid by the day, never entered his head. All that mattered was that they were not ill treated. And he countered the accusation of ostentatiousness by quoting the theologians of Salamanca. According to this learned body, slave owners should not be judged by their ownership of slaves but by their treatment of them. Don Hernando was rather fond of quoting the theologians of Salamanca, as if they were a single entity, particularly when their views coincided with his own.

The slave was a handsome Ethiopian by the name of Eusebio. He was so strong that he could single-handedly pull a cart out of the ditch and hold it up while the wheel was changed. Until young Gonzalo came to the mansion, it had seemed that Eusebio was good for little more than feats of strength. But Gonzalo took a liking to him and set about teaching him to read. As we shall see, this had far-reaching consequences.

Gonzalo was given a room in a shop, normally used as a store and accounts office, next door to the mansion. The mulatto woman, Potenciana, was his servant in these quarters. This was how his acquaintance with the two slaves began.

Gonzalo was in Don Hernando's debt. His father had died safe in the knowledge that he, Gonzalo, would not be destitute. He therefore took great care with the accounts, staying up all night if necessary, to keep the books to the head of the family's satisfaction.

Don Hernando soon discovered his nephew's worth and gave him more responsibility in the administration of his affairs. His duties required him to travel to the extremities of the business, mainly in Ávila, Arévalo, Peñaranda, Madrigal de las Altas Torres and Toledo. These journeys often required him to take money with him. On these occasions Eusebio would accompany him for protection. It was during the long journeys by mule or horse that Gonzalo discerned the first gleams of the African's mind.

At that time the mule was prized above all other animals. Mules were reserved for bishops and other clerical dignitaries. And though it was thought more appropriate for gentlemen to use horses or donkeys, according to their station, it was not considered demeaning for high-ranking civil servants to travel by mule. Don Hernando had four mules. Occasionally, as a sign of his high regard for his nephew, he would let Gonzalo use one of them. As it was forbidden under the so-called Old Law for slaves to ride, Eusebio would stride by his master's side, and when going downhill he would run.

When Gonzalo lost his father and his inheritance, he also lost some of his youthfulness. He became melancholic, and there was more than a touch of the dreamer about him. He thought deeply about things like the futility of trying to get on and making money. He even considered taking holy orders once he had repaid his debt to his uncle.

On long journeys he followed the canon's advice to avoid inns and would stay at convents or monasteries. He was so captivated by the tranquillity of these enclaves of the Kingdom of God that he needed little persuasion. One winter's night a strange thing happened while he was talking about his sorrows and dreams to a venerable Benedictine from the monastery of Los Toros de Guisando.

"Those who seek physic for their hurts in the rigor of monastic life", the old monk began, "find little comfort therein. For we come here not to be healed, but to love. And how can he love whose heart has been hardened by the affairs of this tough world? Take your father's ruin, for instance, which you hold as the greatest of calamities. Is it not in truth of little or no importance? Indeed, is it not actually a blessing? For has it not made you repent your life thus far, so saving your immortal soul? When all is said and done, my son, this is all that really matters."

"I have come to the same conclusion, Father", Gonzalo replied. "But is it not easier to find salvation through a pious life in a monastery than a virtuous life in the world?"

"No, my son. Entering a monastery without being called to do so by God is little better than knocking at the doors of hell itself. When you speak of a virtuous life in the world, you hit the mark. That is the way to salvation, as you put it. And by that way God stands, holding His hand out to you with as much love in His heart as for the friar in his cell. It is my belief", the old Benedictine continued, gravely regarding him, "that you will not enter a monastery but make a good marriage. Not in the eyes of this fickle world, perhaps, but in God's eyes. And there is nothing more pleasing to Our Lord than that which springs from a blessed union."

At these prophetic words, Gonzalo experienced a surge of emotion that, though he did not understand it at the time, took shape in his mind as an image of a young woman with dark eyes and dark hair who was waiting for him in some distant and unknown place.

"What should I do then, Father?" he said at last as he tried to make sense of what he was feeling.

"Be guided by the noblest prompting of your heart. And treat others as you would be treated by them."

It was the harshest winter in memory, and the following morning found the Castilian landscape under a foot or more of snow. One of the most central principles in Don Hernando's code of honor was the prompt settling of accounts. Undeterred by the snow, Gonzalo and Eusebio set off on the next leg of their journey to Ávila to settle such an account.

Gonzalo was riding slowly on one of Don Hernando's mules. Its hooves, which were wrapped in woolen rags against the cold, made next to no sound. Eusebio trudged by his side. The snow was so deep that in places he was sinking in up to his knees. The sight of the slave wading through the snow leading the mule by the bridle touched Gonzalo. Though it had stopped snowing, he told Eusebio to walk in the animal's tracks, so that he did not sink so much into the snow. In spite of this, and the man's prodigious strength, it was heavy going for him and he was soon shivering. Considering where he came from and how difficult he would have found it to get used to the cold of a Castilian winter, this was not surprising.

Still pondering the monk's mysterious words, Gonzalo scanned the snow-covered landscape, shielding his eyes with his hand. It was bitterly cold. There was not another living soul to be seen. He dismounted and ordered his man to mount. Eusebio refused. He might be spotted by a passing patrol. It was strictly forbidden for one of his race. But Gonzalo insisted. He not only made the African get up onto the mule but wrapped him in his cloak, which both warmed and enveloped the rider from head to toe so that he could not be seen.

As Gonzalo set off walking in the mule's tracks, he felt such a deep sense of inner well-being that he began to wonder whether God was not at work in this. He felt neither cold nor tired. And to his surprise he found he could easily keep up with the mule, walking with an energy he rarely had under much easier conditions.

That night, a bitterly cold night with a biting wind, they stopped at a wayside inn. When they were alone in the hayloft, Eusebio fell to his knees. And with tears in his eyes he began to kiss Gonzalo's hands in gratitude. From that day a friendship sprang up between the two men, though they kept it to themselves. Gonzalo soon discovered that the slave could not only speak; he was teaching himself to read.

Throughout the Iberian Peninsula there were two types of African slaves: *ladinos* and *bozales*. *Ladinos* were second-generation slaves who were baptized and spoke Spanish. *Bozales*, having only recently arrived from Africa, spoke barely a word of Spanish. As a result, they were considered inferior and did not fetch such a high price in the marketplace.

Eusebio was a *bozal* from Ethiopia. He understood orders well enough but limited his replies to "Yes, master". It had consequently been supposed that this was all he could say. When he confided in Gonzalo, he confessed that he had picked up a lot from his wife, Potenciana, a *ladina* who spoke perfect Castilian. He had kept it quiet, however, in case Don Hernando should be tempted to sell him. This fear was not entirely unfounded. The natives of the Caribbean proved to have little stomach for gold mining and tilling the fields. The solution was to send out slaves, Spanish-speaking *ladinos* fetching the best prices. Many slave traders, particularly those from Portugal and the Huelva region in Andalusia, imported slaves from the Barbary coast for next to nothing, taught them Spanish and sold them at a handsome profit for the plantations of the Antilles. Don Hernando would occasionally say only half in jest that this would not be a bad business to get into. It was for this reason that Gonzalo did not try to prevail on Eusebio to reveal his secret.

Gonzalo was an avid reader. On the long journeys he would read either religious works or chivalric romances for light entertainment. He would often read aloud, especially the religious works. It occurred to him that this might be a good way to teach the slave the principles of the Catholic faith, of which, despite being baptized, he was profoundly ignorant. Once, when they stopped to rest in the shade of some trees by the side of the road, he picked up a stick and scratched some letters in the dust. At first, it had just been to pass the time, or as a kind of quiz. But when he saw how quickly Eusebio caught on, he began to do it in earnest. It seemed to him miraculous that a person who as far as he could tell had received no kind of education whatever should learn so quickly. The first thing he taught Eusebio was the Hail Mary, Gonzalo being deeply devoted to the Blessed Virgin.

He was touching on an important issue. The discovery of the Indies had sparked a controversy about whether or not the natives had souls. There were plenty of people who wanted to establish that they did not, because it enabled them to treat the natives like animals. A royal edict, endorsed by the Pope, that declared that they did have souls did little to dispel this view. Even if they did have souls, they were surely inferior to those of *cristianos viejos*. And if the Caribbean natives had no souls, or at best inferior souls, would Africans be any different? African slaves were consequently given the most menial tasks, their masters claiming that they were good for little else.

It was for this reason that Gonzalo was so eager for Eusebio to learn to read. He believed reading to be a function of the intellect, and the intellect to be a faculty of the rational soul. But pleased as he was with his discovery, they agreed to say nothing about it to Don Hernando until they had weighed up all the implications.

Potenciana had been a slave all her life and was not dissatisfied with her lot. So they decided to say nothing to her either. Her worst fear was that her husband would do something rash that would result in their fortunes taking a turn for the worse. Nevertheless, she was grateful to Gonzalo for the kindness he had shown them, and on their return from a journey she took him aside.

"Master," she began, "I have it on good authority that Don Hernando is very pleased with you. So pleased with you indeed that he has decided to wed you to one of his daughters. Which it is to be, however, he has not yet decided."

The "good authority" turned out to be the ear she was in the habit of pressing to the keyhole.

This news troubled Gonzalo. His apprehension only deepened when Don Hernando told him he was to quit his cramped lodgings in the accounts office and move into the big house. One of the best rooms in the house, a beautiful, sunny room in the eaves, had been made ready for him. And from then on, whenever he was in Medina, he was to eat with the family.

As already mentioned, Don Hernando had four daughters, ranging from eighteen to twenty-five years in age. It could not exactly be said that they were unattractive. They were poised and dressed in silks. All were accomplished clavichord players. But somehow they remained undistinguished by any special quality. Their mother, though pliant to her husband, was a woman of indomitable character and commanded respect in her own right.

Gonzalo was nearly twenty-one. He was not unaware that

a penniless orphan would be fortunate indeed to make such an advantageous match. What troubled him was his suspicion that Potenciana's news was nothing less than the truth. And the change in his uncle's behavior toward him only confirmed this. But which one would it be? His uncertainty about that was even more disquieting.

He was quite fond of the eldest daughter, with whom he shared a love of books. They would exchange volumes and discuss them. His cousins were not unfriendly toward him. Indeed, they treated him like an equal. But he could not say he loved any of them, though he was not sure about this because he did not know what love was. When he allowed his mind to dwell on the thought of his conjugal duties, and with which of his cousins he would most like to fulfill them, he would blush.

"Suppose, dear boy," Don Hernando began one evening a little in his cups after a good dinner, "you were to take a fancy to one of your cousins . . . with a view to marriage, of course", he added hastily, glancing at his wife. "And suppose you were to think that our kinship meant you would need a dispensation . . . Not so. Our common ancestor is a great-grandfather. This puts our consanguinity at the tenth level, and to this the Church has no objection."

Don Hernando had shown his hand at last. He would have pursued the matter then and there if his wife had not interjected dryly that this was no way to speak in front of young ladies. That night Don Hernando and his wife had words. The following day Potenciana had more information for Gonzalo.

"If it was up to Don Hernando," she began, "you would marry the eldest, and that would be that. For whomever she marries will inherit the business one day. And there is none who knows the business better than you, master, none who works harder, or would run it half as well as you, for all our sakes."

"Does it make no difference, then," the young man wondered aloud, "that I have not a *maravedí* to my name, that there is not a thing in the world I can call my own but my debt to my benefactor?"

"No, master. In fact, it is in your favor. I overheard him talking to my lady. Not only are you in his debt, you are a man of honor. So you will do what you are told. A son-in-law with his own fortune might not be so bound. What the master desires above all is control of the business and all in it. The cause of their dispute was that the eldest has a long-standing suitor with his own fortune whom she favors. And my lady sees no reason to gainsay her. So you had better look to María, though I am not sure about that either."

María, the second daughter, was very sweet but a bit of a dreamer. She was prone to trancelike raptures that were not uncommon at that time. It later emerged that these were caused by a longing to enter religious life.

By the spring of 1528, Gonzalo was fairly sure he was intended for the third daughter, Andrea. On feast days, while Don Hernando took his siesta, the family would stroll in a copse by a stream that ran into the Duero. Then Gonzalo would find himself paired off with Andrea, who was his own age and not unattractive. With an innocent air, she would glance around and, taking his hand, make suggestive remarks about conjugal relations. Feigning no more than a cousin's interest, she studied his palm, as if reading his fortune. This would invariably end in his marriage to a girl so like herself that Gonzalo would blush. He was neither flirtatious by nature nor so prudish as to be offended by it.

Potenciana confirmed that Andrea was the one. She, for

her part, seemed delighted with the arrangement. Gonzalo set about returning her feelings, earnestly thinking about marriage and even reading some classical literature on the subject of love. Then something happened that is seldom written about in books, something that swept away all his doubts like a torrent. It happened in Fontiveros, a small town a dozen miles or so from Medina.

Chapter 3

Love in Fontiveros

In the village of La Moraña near Fontiveros lived a widow with a small weaving workshop. She is known simply as the widow of La Moraña and appears as such in Don Hernando's ledgers. Modest though the business was, she kept up her payments and was consequently regarded by the Yepeses as a model customer. "Little and often fills the purse", they would say, wagging their fingers. Wherever possible, the Yepeses avoided doing business with the upper classes. The nobility had few scruples about being slow to settle their debts, or about settling them at all. Not so the poor, with whom the bailiffs were less lenient.

Gonzalo had gone to Fontiveros to settle the account of the widow of La Moraña. The next day he went to Mass in a small Carmelite convent. It was already hot, and he rose early to hear Mass in the cool of morning, intending to push on toward Arévalo afterward.

As is the custom in Carmelite convents, the church was in semidarkness. Feeling a cool breeze from an open window, he moved toward it and found himself standing next to a young woman who had had the same idea. As he neared her she turned, and their eyes met in the half-light. She smiled, inclining her head slightly. It was not a bold smile but a smile of recognition, the gesture of a devout person in a sacred place. Whenever there was an opportunity during the

Mass he studied her out of the corner of his eye, curious to know who she was and how it was that she seemed to know him. He could not place her. Yet with every glance he was more and more struck by her serenity, the delicacy of her features and the devotion with which she followed the Sacrifice of the Mass. A lace mantilla partly covered her face, which only added to her mystique. Though respectable, she was not dressed like a lady. Nor was she dressed like a poor person. Her pink, finely shaped lips moved silently as she followed the office in a worn little prayer book.

As soon as Mass finished she hurried out of the church, bending her head again as she slipped past Gonzalo. He wanted to follow her but did not dare. He had to content himself with returning her nod. His feelings were in turmoil. All that day and on those that followed, his unsettled state continued. He changed his plans so as to be in the Carmelite convent at the same time the following week. He was not disappointed. There she was, standing by the window as before, with her mantilla and her worn little prayer book. And she looked so surprised to see him again that he did not know what to make of it. Nor did he know what to make of his own feelings, except that they were very different from those that Andrea's pouting smiles evoked in him.

He had been unable to get the young woman out of his mind all week. And yet he knew next to nothing about her. Why, he wondered, was it so important to him to find out who she was? And how was it that she seemed to know him? He decided that the next day, Monday, he would go and see the widow, who was bound to know all the inhabitants of Fontiveros.

He did not have to wait long for the answers to these questions. As he entered the widow's workshop the following morning, he saw the young woman. She was sitting by a tiny window with her back to him. A long tress of black hair hung down her back. She was wearing a head scarf of the kind worn by weavers to protect their hair from the lanolin. Her hands moved deftly over the loom. Hearing someone come in, she turned and smiled, just as she had done in the church. Had she smiled at him like that on previous occasions when he had come in, he wondered? If so, he had not noticed her until their providential meeting in the Carmelite convent that sultry Sunday morning in August. Her head scarf and the long smock she wore could hardly have been less flattering. Still, Gonzalo could not understand how he had failed to notice her striking dark eyes and delicate profile. As he pondered this, he suddenly remembered the strange feeling that had come over him in his conversation with the old Benedictine.

Her name was Catalina Alvarez. When both her parents died, leaving her a pauper, she was adopted by the widow, who had been a good friend of theirs. Her father had been a scribe in the office of the curia in Toledo. She had grown up in that city and had even received some education there.

The following Sunday Gonzalo again went to the Carmelite convent to hear Mass. As if by prearrangement, Catalina was waiting for him at the door. They exchanged a few words and went in together. After Mass he walked her to the widow's house. The widow did not try to hide the girl's many excellent qualities, little imagining Gonzalo's true feelings. It was common knowledge that he was highly regarded by Don Hernando and was to marry one of his daughters. But with every word the widow spoke, Gonzalo's ardor grew until his life became a kind of living death.

He began to travel the dozen or so miles between Medina and Fontiveros whenever possible, arranging all his journeys so as to pass through the village. At first the widow thought he had dishonorable intentions. It was not uncommon for young men from the towns who were about to enter into an arranged marriage to seduce peasant girls. Catalina would not have been the first weaver to have given up her virtue to a young merchant, only to be left standing at the altar.

"You will not dishonor her, sir, if I can help it", the widow avowed. "She is little more than a child, so innocent and trusting that her very life depends on that trust. She deserves a better fate. No, you will not dishonor her, sir."

"Rest assured, good widow", he replied. "To me Catalina is like a dream from another world. I would sooner take my own life than dishonor a single hair on her head, though I would go straight to hell for it, which God forbid."

"What do you want, then?" the widow asked in alarm. "You surely do not intend to marry her?"

It was not that she disliked Gonzalo. It was simply inconceivable to her that he should wish to marry her ward.

"I do", he replied.

"Sir, you are from a rich and powerful family. She is a penniless orphan, ignorant of all but the twilling of worsted. I ask you, sir, in whose interests would such a marriage be? Not mine, I assure you. I am a poor widow. My livelihood depends on this humble workshop. What would become of me if I were to bring the weight of Don Hernando's wrath upon my head? The Yepeses supply me with my raw materials on trust. If I lose that trust, I am ruined . . ."

With these impassioned words the widow began to weep.

"Do not come here again, sir, I beg of you. Leave us alone . . ."

The widow was not a bad woman at heart. Her life had been hard. And though she could see, and was even touched, by the love that had clearly sprung up between the two young people, she believed it to be an infatuation, to which time and common sense would eventually put an end. It was in these terms that she spoke to her ward.

"Forget Gonzalo de Yepes", she urged. "He will not be coming back. His duty is to honor the pledge he has made to Don Hernando Aguilera de Yepes to marry his third daughter."

"That day will never come!" Catalina exclaimed with a vehemence the widow had never seen in her sweet-natured ward before. "No doubt Don Hernando wants him to marry Andrea. But there has been no formal proposition, and Gonzalo has given him no pledge. Besides, a wedding is out of the question, for now at least. Don Hernando intends to marry all his daughters together. But who their husbands are to be has not yet been decided, except that of the second daughter, who is to be Our Lord Jesus Christ."

The widow stared at Catalina. She could not believe they had gotten so far in their talks together. She had never taken her eyes off them during Gonzalo's visits to Fontiveros. Had they really discussed such things in their seemingly innocent exchanges?

"Yes, Aunt, and many more", Catalina replied ardently. "I have not stopped thinking about him since the first time he walked through that door over a year ago now. He did not even know I existed, of course. I made sure of that. Why would a man of his quality notice a poor, plain weaver? But whenever he came in I knew it. My heart would tell me. Yet I did not look up. I would shrink into the corner. From there, unobserved, I feasted my eyes on him as he went over the books with you, glutting myself on every particular of his person—the way he spoke, the light in his eyes, his noble bearing, so that he had only to lift a cup to his lips and I would imagine it to be ambrosia."

The widow listened to this outburst with astonishment.

She had never heard her ward utter so many words at once, or with such passion.

"What are you saying, child?" the widow spluttered, "What are you saying? Have you lost your wits? Come to your senses and be yourself again."

"*He* is my self", Catalina burst out again. "When I saw him walk into the church that first Sunday and come toward me, I thought my heart would fly out of my breast. And when he was there again the following Sunday, I no longer doubted that an angel from Heaven was guiding him to me. Oh Aunt, Aunt, for God's sake, have pity on me!"

With this she burst into tears. Falling to her knees, she put her arms around the widow's waist, clasping her with all her strength. The old woman wept with her because she loved her like a daughter. But she was immovable. The idea of treating the mighty Don Hernando Aguilera de Yepes with disrespect was unthinkable. It would be nothing short of madness.

The widow's decision prostrated Gonzalo. He did not know what to do, or to whom to turn for help. The only person he could think of was the old Benedictine from Los Toros. Short of hoping for some supernatural intervention, he could see no way on earth to overcome the obstacles in his path. Almost mad with a restless yearning, there was only one thing he knew for certain. He loved Catalina, and she loved him. And it was no ordinary love. It was something so pure that it was unlike anything he had come across except in the books of courtly love.

To make up for all his coming and going, he threw himself into his work with redoubled energy. He did so well, indeed, that he won the contract to supply the biggest mill in the area, Cebreros. Don Hernando was delighted, praising him excessively and urging him on. He interpreted Gonzalo's hard work as an attempt to please his prospective father-in-law. When Gonzalo told him about the Cebreros contract, Don Hernando solemnly intoned:

"If you carry on like this, my boy, I will shortly be able to give you something that will not displease you, I think."

Fearing the worst, Gonzalo went to see the old Benedictine to tell him what was going on. But he was in such a state that when he tried to explain it the old monk misunderstood.

"My son," he remonstrated, "it is not normal to fall so suddenly in love. Love is sometimes confused with lust, principally when it comes through the senses. Tell me, my son," he went on in a measured tone, "do your eyes light up when you see her? Are her words music to your ears? Is the scent of her body perfume to your nose? And when you touch her, do certain things happen to your body?"

To each of these questions, Gonzalo answered in the affirmative.

"When I think of her in my waking hours," he went on, "which is as often as the day is long, for I cannot stop thinking about her, I see her as if on a pedestal where no impure thought can touch her. But in my dreams I find that we are already man and wife, if you take my meaning, Father. And then such unspeakably pleasurable things happen to me that when I wake, I am ashamed."

"Do not trouble yourself about that", the old monk replied. "There is no sin where there is neither volition nor consent. But I am troubled that your senses might be playing too strong a part in what you call love. For while these things can be God-given, they can also spring from the devil."

"How can I tell?" Gonzalo asked in alarm.

"Through prayer and self-mortification", the monk replied. "And you may be sure I too shall pray that the Lord may enlighten you."

It did not take Eusebio long to discover that his young master was sticking pins in his breeches to mortify his flesh.

"Have a care, master", he said with a mixture of concern and barely concealed mirth. "That part of the body is exceedingly tender. Indeed, I would say it is better suited to other purposes than reflecting on the state of your immortal soul."

When he had gotten over his own amusement, Gonzalo was struck by the soundness of this reasoning. Since learning the rudiments of the faith through his reading, Eusebio had become a deep thinker. He was a good worker, his immense strength in handling the bales and his cheerful nature having made him a favorite of the weavers.

By this time master and slave had become firm friends. It had been agreed that in open country they would share the horse or mule. They had thus talked a good deal, and Eusebio was well aware of his master's turmoil.

"There is surely no reason to doubt the words of such a wise and virtuous man as the good Benedictine, is there, master?" the slave began one day on the road to Ávila.

"None", Gonzalo replied.

The slave nodded thoughtfully and continued after a moment:

"What he said about love that is born of the senses troubles me. I cannot shake off the idea that my love for Potenciana might come from the devil. For the first time I set eyes on her, the day she came from Lisbon, a heavenly scent seemed to fill the air. And she swears she smelled it too. Yet as God is my witness, I had just been mucking out the pig sty. And the first few times we were together before we were married, which I assure you were as innocent as befits those of little acquaintance, I felt such rare pleasure in her company that it was as if the marrow in my bones would burst into bloom like blossoms.''

And he went on to describe other sensations that made Gonzalo smile, not because of what he said but because of the way he said it. The slave's eloquence delighted him. Here was a man who only two or three months ago had been little more than a simpleton, thought by many to be dumb.

"What conclusion have you come to, then, in all your thinking?" he put in when Eusebio at last paused to draw breath.

"That it was through my senses that I discovered my love for Potenciana. How else? For I did not even know I had a soul until I knew you, master. But thanks to this thrusting on of the senses, we have two children, and there is another on the way. And once baptized, they will become good Christians and bring great glory to God. And now I think I have said enough."

"You say much, condemned slave", Gonzalo replied with a show of anger. "But unless I am mistaken, you have more to say on the matter. Stop beating about the bush and say what is on your mind."

On journeys, which might take days to complete, conversations between travelers were often drawn out. Lengthy pauses between question and answer, sometimes lasting for several miles of the road, were not unusual. The talk might be interspersed with comments about the landscape, exchanges with passing shepherds about the weather, and stops to answer the call of nature, drink from a brook or buy fruit from a wayside garden or grapes from a vineyard. The land thronged with people, each with his own trade—plowman, reaper, gelder, shepherd, farrier, weaver, knife grinder and, of course, robber. For this reason Eusebio always carried a steel-tipped club for self-defense and to guard the money they carried. A reply would always come in the end, however. On this occasion, after much reflection, Eusebio replied:

"You are not mistaken, master. I have been so bold as to venture one or two thoughts of my own, as if my thoughts counted for anything, when I can scarcely scratch my letters in the dust and must use my fingers to count two and two. In this at least, Potenciana has the upper hand. For though she cannot read, or count up to five, she knows the difference between right and wrong. For no sooner do we return from a journey than she begins to ply me with questions about the widow's ward, and issue threats."

"Threats? What threats?"

"Why, that if I lift a finger to help you in this business, it will be the last thing I do, for no good can come of it. And that as a last resort, I am to contrive a fall, or find some means to break your leg, so that you must needs stay in Medina and wed Doña Andrea. So let us have done with this business once and for all, master."

"Says she so indeed?" said Gonzalo, now genuinely angry.

"Yes, master. And more besides. But only because she has our best interests in mind."

Gonzalo fell silent. He knew the slave couple well enough to know that Potenciana was saying white only because Eusebio had said black and that if it came to it, he would prevail. For although he was a good Christian, he was not above taking a stick to his wife, as was the custom in his native Africa. At length Gonzalo inquired:

"And what precisely do you consider your 'best interests' to be?"

"That you wed Doña Andrea. For then would we form part of the dowry. And knowing the esteem in which you hold me, master, of which God knows I am unworthy, she can already see me as steward of the business. Moreover, she is so bold as to dream that in your will you might grant me my liberty. And, though it would be of little use to me, nor do I ask it, it being a blessing to be your slave, she rightly says that in that case our children would be free. It is for this reason that she desires you to wed Doña Andrea, master."

The fire in the slave's eye and the passion in his words brought a lump into Gonzalo's throat.

"Is that the only reason?" he succeeded in asking after a pause.

"No, master. Doña Andrea is a fine young lady. She is attached to you. It would be a tidy dowry. And, who knows, you might inherit the whole business one day . . ."

They were on a road that followed the course of a stream that runs from the Endramada to Ramacastañas. The trees on either side of this stream providing some cover, Eusebio was in the saddle while Gonzalo strode along at his side. It was a fine, clear day and the ground was lush with fresh grass and marsh marigolds, as always in that part of the world when the sun returns after the autumn rains.

"And what do you think? Do you agree with Potenciana?" Gonzalo inquired.

"Potenciana knows only Doña Andrea. She does not know Doña Catalina."

"Well?"

"I know both of them."

Eusebio reined in.

"Begging your pardon, master, it does not seem right to me that I should be up here proffering opinions while you walk, as if you were the slave and I the master. Mount, master, and I shall walk."

They argued the point, debating the worth of one man in relation to another. In the end they decided to rest the horse, an ill-tempered nag but the best the previous post had had to offer, and go on together on foot.

"It is not my place", the slave began again, "to compare their qualities. But unless I am much deceived, I can see this —that while Doña Andrea's company is not exactly irksome to you, when you are with Doña Catalina, you fall into a kind of reverie that is not of this world. Or so it seems to me. And she likewise, except that in your case, your bottom lip gapes, which, begging your pardon master—does you no favors, whereas the effect upon her is to make her even more beautiful than she already is. And I do believe that in this state she could fly up to Heaven if she so wished. And if this were the devil's work, I doubt not your meetings would be attended by a sulfurous smell, or some such thing. Yet when you are together, even the widow is transported, though it plainly troubles her. As for me, for all my ignorance and stupidity, I too feel something akin to this when I am with Potenciana . . ."

"Enough!" Gonzalo interrupted. "You will repeat what you have said word for word to the good Benedictine of Los Toros."

And with a firm tug on the bridle, they turned and set off for the monastery by way of Monbeltrán and Santa Cruz del Valle.

The slave Eusebio made such an impression on the venerable monk that the reason for their visit was forgotten. He was fascinated by the slave. He wanted to know how he had come by his learning, who his teacher had been and the method of his instruction. Eusebio's knowledge delighted him. It seemed to him to prove that we are all God's children and that knowledge has nothing whatever to do with the color of our skin but with the extent to which we take advantage of the opportunities presented to each of us by the Creator.

"If you teach your own children half so well," he said, turning to Gonzalo, "your marriage will be a great blessing to many people."

"God hear your words, Reverend Father", Gonzalo replied. "But if I might put Your Reverence in mind of the reason for our coming, to whom should that marriage be?"

"I believe your slave has more to say on that score than I", the old monk replied. "I can only repeat what I said at our first meeting. Be guided by the noblest prompting of your heart. And may God forgive me for ever thinking the devil might have had anything to do with this."

They left the monastery with the old monk's blessing. Once again they took the road to Ávila by way of Fontiveros. For Eusebio had left his young master in no doubt that although the baser part of his nature whispered in his ear, urging him to persuade Gonzalo to marry Andrea and lead a life of security and prosperity, every fiber of the nobler part of his being clamored for the widow's ward.

"Have no fear, master, I share your feelings with all my heart. But I think it would be best to say nothing of this to Potenciana, for she has base instincts, and dreams of little else but your marriage to Doña Andrea, so that under your protection we might get on."

They went straight to the widow's workshop without stopping to rest. With great solemnity, Gonzalo asked for Catalina's hand. The widow flatly refused, muttered a string of oaths and slammed the door in his face.

That night, according to the custom in such circumstances, with the help of the slave Eusebio, Gonzalo abducted Catalina and deposited her in a convent of nuns of the Order of Saint Clare in Peñaranda del Bracamonte. Having supplied them with cloth and always having treated them respectfully, he was very highly though of by them. Then, with the widow's shrill voice ringing in his ears, he returned to Medina at a gallop to inform Don Hernando of his decision.

Chapter 4

The Joyous Workshop

The rage of the head of the family was far worse than anything Gonzalo had imagined. But at last Don Hernando seemed to regain his self-control and began to listen to Gonzalo's explanation.

When he had finished, there was a long silence.

"So", he began at last. "It may not be too late. You say there has been no marriage? No betrothal, no dowry pledge with the lady in question?"

"No, sir."

"Good. All is not lost. It would not be the first time that a Yepes has slaked his thirst, so to speak, before entering into a marriage of substance with his intended."

"Sir," Gonzalo replied, "my feelings for the lady have little or nothing to do with my 'thirst', as you put it, but with my heart and my soul."

"A pox on your heart and soul!" said Don Hernando, his face darkening again. "In these situations the flesh deceives the soul, and vice versa. Indulge your fancy in both respects if you must. What I am trying to tell you is that as long as you keep it within the bounds of moderation and don't go prating about it, I see no reason why it should stand in the way of your marriage to my daughter."

Gonzalo did not reply. He could not understand what his uncle was proposing. When he did finally understand, he did not even have the strength to be outraged.

"Sir, with all due respect," he began again with tears in his eyes, "I cannot marry your daughter because I love another. If, as I beg you to do, you will consent to my marriage to the young lady in question, whom I love with all my heart and with all my soul, I will vow to be your most faithful servant."

"You reap what you sow", Don Hernando thundered in reply. "Your father died a pauper because he cut himself off from the Yepeses. And I'll be damned if I don't see to it that you go the same way. Out of my sight!"

That night Gonzalo slept in a barn outside the city walls. He had tried to go into the house to speak to Andrea but had found the door locked and his few belongings lying on the ground outside. At dusk the following day, one of Don Hernando's clerks came in secret to the barn. The old clerk, a *converso* [a converted Jew] and a skilled bookkeeper, liked Gonzalo. He told him that Don Hernando had ordered the books of every account Gonzalo had ever handled to be gone through with a fine-tooth comb, and that if a single *maravedí* was missing, he would have Gonzalo arrested and thrown into jail.

"I know they will find nothing", the man said. "You are not like the others. You are an honest man. But take care. Do not linger here. If I were you, I would put some distance between myself and this place."

Gonzalo thanked him. Early the next morning, as he was preparing to put the old clerk's advice into practice, Potenciana showed up. She was all disheveled, her hair loose, and there was a wild look in her eye. It seemed Don Hernando had found out about her husband's part in the abduction and removal of the widow's ward. After having him flogged, he had sent Eusebio to a remote hill farm to tend goats until he could find a Portuguese slave trader who shipped slaves to the Indies.

Mortified though Gonzalo was by this news, he could not help his heart leaping. In spite of everything, he was going to marry Catalina, even if they too would have to emigrate to the Indies.

As soon as Gonzalo set eyes on Potenciana, he had a feeling he was about to find out what Eusebio had meant about her having "base instincts".

"What is so improper about what the master proposes?" she began indignantly. "Do you think it unusual for young men to seek pleasure in the arms of girls before marriage? I tell you it is not. If you mean to impress the master with your high principles, think again. For on our way from Lisbon where he bought me, he forced himself upon me. And I . . ."

At this the unfortunate woman began to weep.

Gonzalo was rendered speechless for a moment by this heartbreaking revelation.

"Potenciana," he gently began, "all I can do is give you my word that I will do my utmost to help Eusebio. More than this I cannot do."

"You can, sir", the wretched woman sobbed. "You can marry the master's daughter. For if you do not, you will shortly be clapped in irons. Of that you can be certain. And what could you do then?"

News of Don Hernando's anger had run through the big house like wildfire. Gonzalo was anxious to leave as soon as possible. But, though he knew he was taking a big risk, he was determined not to go before speaking to Andrea, the only person to whom he felt he owed an explanation.

He asked Potenciana if she knew of any way for him to meet Andrea. Seizing this opportunity, as she saw it, to put things right, she arranged a meeting in the grove of poplars by the river.

Andrea came chaperoned by an ancient nurse, who stood a little way off. With a tilt of her chin, Andrea fixed him with a look that would have curdled milk. Before Gonzalo could say a word, she began loftily, "Sir, I gather the attentions you were so gracious as to confer upon me were nothing to those you bestow upon a village girl, whose name I cannot bring myself to utter."

Gonzalo stared at her, dumbfounded.

"Have you anything to say, sir?"

"Andrea," he stammered, "if anyone was gracious, it was you. It was an honor to be admitted into your society. You have been a true friend, and I would not lose that friendship for the world. If I have offended you in any way, I beg your pardon with all my heart."

"Who would be offended by the attentions of such a gentleman?" she replied with sudden laughter in her eyes. "What offense could a lady take at such a thing?"

Gonzalo and Andrea had always liked each other. Her feelings toward him might have gone further than this. But it had always bothered her eldest sister that Andrea was to marry one of their father's employees. So she had done her best to put Andrea off, talking incessantly about a cousin of her fiancé's who was soon to be a *comendador* and would be a much better match. She, at least, had been delighted by the news of Gonzalo's fall from favor and had done her best to persuade her younger sister that it was for the best.

Andrea stopped pretending to be angry and began to ply Gonzalo with questions about how he had found a love for which he was prepared to give up the many advantages of belonging to the Yepes family. And, when he described the moment when he first saw Catalina, Andrea heaved a deep sigh, her eyes glistening.

Andrea told him in no uncertain terms that her father would never forgive the insult. But her forgiveness meant a great deal to Gonzalo. As if endowed with prophetic powers, she went on to tell him that his reward would be not only in this world but in the next. She was not mistaken.

Andrea Aguilera de Yepes married the man her sister had wanted for her. He turned out to be a young man with many good qualities. They fell truly in love and had five sons, each more accomplished than the others. One of them professed his vows in the Carmelite Order and was one of Fray Juan's most faithful followers in the Reform of the Order. Andrea, by then a wealthy widow, endowed a monastery of Discalced Carmelites near Peñuela in the province of Jaén. Throughout her life she was proud of once having been courted by the man who was to become the father of San Juan de la Cruz (Saint John of the Cross). She was often heard to say she was not surprised that a love as pure as that between her cousin and Catalina Alvarez should have produced such a saintly son. Andrea died at the age of ninety in full command of her faculties, admired by all who knew her, not least for her sense of humor, which she never lost.

The devil himself would not have received a colder reception from the widow of La Moraña than Gonzalo did. Not only had he taken away her ward, but she was staring ruin in the face. News of Don Hernando's fury and his intention to clap Gonzalo in irons had reached Fontiveros.

"An honest man can always be brought down one way or another", the old clerk had intoned. "Even if every last *maravedí* in your books is accounted for, I expect they'll find one or two missing somewhere else."

Gonzalo resigned himself to emigrating. He decided to go to the Indies in the employ of a merchant from Ávila who owned land on the islands of Hispaniola and Cuba. Cuba had not yet been fully explored and was thought to be a continent. Such fabulous things were said about it, indeed, that some people believed it to have been Eden.

The merchant, whose name was Nicomedes, had a high opinion of Gonzalo. He told him that with very little effort he could be rich. But he advised Gonzalo not to go stumbling about the jungle searching for gold and silver, for such riches were easily lost, almost always ending up in the hands of unscrupulous traders and pirates. Nicomedes himself had started out in the Indies as a cloth merchant. He had subsequently gone into gold and silver and had also dabbled in the slave trade.

When Gonzalo told the widow that he had decided to emigrate to the Indies, she promptly fainted. To her it might as well have been the far side of the moon. At long last she had realized what she felt for her ward, a love as deep as if she had been her own daughter, and the thought of her going away, maybe forever, brought her to the brink of death.

Catalina, meanwhile, was patiently waiting in the convent of Peñaranda del Bracamonte, praying that Gonzalo would find a way to get to the altar and the Indies. But news of the widow's reaction, and the thought that she might inadvertently cause her adopted mother's death, troubled her deeply. She left her refuge and returned to the workshop, her home for so many years, resigned to giving up her marriage if she must.

"If you do that, my child," said the prioress, "you will regret it for the rest of your days. Take care, for the devil likes nothing better than a broken heart. Of all the ways to damnation, it is the quickest."

The prioress, Reverend Mother Agueda of the Heart of Christ, was a resolute woman with a deep understanding of human nature. She decided to accompany Catalina to her home and speak to the widow. But the widow would not listen to her.

"Leave me alone", the widow wailed, wringing her hands. "Let me die in peace."

"Die you must", the prioress replied. "But you can still do so in peace. For you may be sure that you will have precious little in the life to come if you die with this on your conscience, that you stood in the way of a love as pure as that in the Song of Songs."

"Do you speak of hell?" the widow replied with a great start.

"One whose fear of a mere mortal is greater than that of God deserves no less. For it seems to me that, in your terror of the name of Yepes, you hinder God's will."

At that time reverence for God's ordained servants was almost as great as the fear of hell. When the widow finally understood what the prioress was saying, she sprang up from the bed on which she had been lying prostrate for days.

"Whatever you say", the widow stammered. "The wedding. We must prepare for the wedding. Name the day, let there be no delay; but for pity's sake, take me with you to the Indies, for if you leave me here, I am done for."

The wedding took place in a small church on calle de Cantiveros on June 28, 1529, the feast of Saint Irenaeus, one of the first theologians of the Church. A member of the congregation was later to give the following account of the event:

> The beauty, purity and poise of the bride, Catalina Alvarez, were not of this world. To witness the ineffable moment of her marriage to such a fine gentleman was like what one might suppose the angels in Heaven experience when they come before our Maker. Her bearing proclaimed her to be of noble birth. None would have guessed that she was a

simple weaver, for those of that lowly trade tend to have rough, even calloused, hands, whereas hers were soft and without blemish of any kind. Yet though her bearing won the admiration of many, her love won the heart of all. As for the bridegroom, he was in a transport of ecstasy. And when the priest pronounced them husband and wife in the sight of God and man, he could not prevent a sob escaping his lips because of all that had gone before. He was not alone in being so moved. After the wedding, there was a modest celebration. This was provided by a wealthy merchant from Ávila who was intending to send Gonzalo de Yepes across the ocean. In this, as it turned out, he did not succeed.

He did not succeed because when Don Hernando had gotten over the first shock of what Gonzalo had done, he saw things more clearly. He concluded that the dishonor that the imprisonment of a Yepes would bring on the family would not be in its best interests. But he could not forgive the insult. He forbade the family to have anything to do with Gonzalo, to write to him or to communicate with him in any way that implied friendship. And he issued a similar embargo to all merchants with whom the family had any dealings.

This effectively put an end to any chance Gonzalo might have had of getting on. With his contractual and bookkeeping skills, he would easily have found work from other artisans in the area, among whom he was well known. But it was not in their interests to get on the wrong side of the Yepeses. Nor would Gonzalo have put them in such a position. So the possibility of going out to the Indies again arose. Every time the subject came up, however, the widow went to pieces. She would tell them to go. They were young and should leave her to die and be buried in her birthplace.

"Why not go out to the Indies on your own?" she said to Gonzalo one day. "Then, in time, when you are settled, you can send for us both."

"If all the riches of Tamerlane were there," he replied, "I would not exchange an hour, a minute, a second with my Catalina for them. When I married her, I thought I loved her. But what a poor thing that was compared to what I now feel."

The discovery that Catalina was pregnant had put Gonzalo into a state of ecstasy. He made a resolution that he kept for the rest of his life, never again to worry about money or commerce, or to put up with the discomfort of the road. Instead, he would live a quiet life in the bosom of his family. This, he now knew, was to be close to God. He immediately set about learning the trade of weaver, which was not considered fitting work for a man, let alone a man of his lineage and education.

He did not care when some of his friends laughed at him. Time was to prove his decision a good one. It was not long before other men in Fontiveros followed suit and took up the trade of weaver.

The widow's workshop was not small. But it was inefficiently laid out. The looms stood higgledy-piggledy around an open-fire kitchen range that tainted the bundles of wool with cooking smells. And, as the widow kept the windows tightly shut, the atmosphere was unbearably stuffy.

Gonzalo wanted to divide the house into two halves: living quarters and a light, airy workplace. The widow agreed to his plans as long as he and Catalina did not go to the Indies. He began the work with the help of Eusebio, who was still banished. Potenciana kept up her attempts to get her husband back, constantly reminding Gonzalo by letter and messenger of his promise to help. Eusebio's fear that they would be sold at any moment grew as he waited on his rocky hilltop. The idea that Gonzalo's situation was not much better than theirs and that he was effectively powerless never entered Potenciana's mind.

One day Catalina went to see the prioress who had been so good to her at the time of her marriage. It seemed the prioress knew of a prelate with a large estate in Muñosancho on the road from Peñaranda to Fontiveros. The estate had been allowed to deteriorate. It was not that the prelate was lazy, exactly. He had continued to carry out the basic requirements of his ministry, but he was studious. He had spent much of his life studying Nebrija. His greatest ambition was to publish an article challenging Nebrija's theory of versification and the syllable in volume 2 of his *Gramática*. Indeed, the prelate had become so obsessed with this that the nuns of Peñaranda had been obliged to step in and look after him. In return, he served Mass for them without stipend.

"I think I may have found just the thing for Your Reverence", the resourceful prioress said to him one day. "An African slave couple. They would take care of the estate and see to Your Reverence's needs."

"Reverend Mother!" the prelate exclaimed. "An ordained priest a slave owner? What will you think of next!"

"Isn't every sister in this community already Your Reverence's slave?" the prioress replied. "Slaves are slaves only if treated as such."

She went on to describe the hardship Eusebio and his family were going through. The prelate was sympathetic to this. What interested him, however, was her claim that the slave could read and write. To see if this was true, he agreed to the priores' suggestion.

The prioress, and the sister charged with the administration of the community, went to Medina del Campo to arrange for the purchase of the slave Eusebio and his wife. She told Don Hernando that she wanted to buy the slaves for a prelate by the name of Anastasio Sifuentes who was going out to the Indies.

Don Hernando agreed to sell Eusebio. Not Potenciana, however. But the *señora*, whose mild manner masked a formidable will, said they must be sold together with their children. It would be cruel to part them. Even if she did not know what her husband had done, she may well have had her suspicions.

The arrival of the slave couple did wonders for the prelate's life. From then on his soutanes were always clean and pressed, he ate his meals at the proper time and he even put on a bit of weight, which made him a more imposing figure when carrying out his sacred duties.

The estate also benefited. Eusebio planted crops, fruit and vegetables beside a stream. He was helped by Potenciana and the eldest child, who was now ten. Though the boy was of mixed race, probably Don Hernando's son, Eusebio treated him as his own. There was so much work that at harvest time they had to take on two laborers.

Great as this improvement was, the prelate was most delighted by Eusebio's penmanship. The slave copied out his work in a hand that a court scrivener could not have bettered. The prelate would occasionally take Eusebio with him to the cathedral in Ávila to show the canons that he was not exaggerating his skill. He was so pleased with Eusebio, indeed, that he dictated an instruction setting the whole slave family free upon his death.

When Gonzalo began rebuilding the workshop, Eusebio would walk the ten miles from Muñosancho to Fontiveros at night to help him.

At last the workshop was finished. With the sun streaming in through the large windows, Gonzalo would weave beside his wife, watching his children grow. He found such contentment in this that he professed himself the happiest of men and said he would not have changed places with anyone, not even the emperor of China. His poetry was now always about the simple life and about those who walk with God. At mealtimes he would bless the food with deep veneration. He could think of no greater blessing than to receive his daily bread, even if it was only barley bread. The couple were grateful for whatever they could put on the table and often invited the poor in to eat with them.

Their first child, Francisco, was born in June 1530. Francisco might not have achieved the renown of his younger brother Juan, but he is regarded by some to have been no less saintly. It is generally acknowledged that Juan's sanctity was at least in part due to Francisco's example. And Francisco in his turn was shaped by his father, Gonzalo, whose way of life was his guiding light until the age of thirteen, when Gonzalo died.

Gonzalo, who had never shown much skill with his hands, made Francisco's crib himself. He was extremely proud of it. It was so good, indeed, that a lady wanted to buy it. He would not part with it, however. He offered to make another one, but it did not turn out as well.

Their second son was born the following year. All we know about him is that his name was Luis and that he died in infancy. Eleven years were to pass before Juan was born. By then Gonzalo and Catalina were beginning to lose hope of having any more children. The birth was miraculously

painless. Catalina said the Blessed Virgin could not have
had an easier time. But even as Catalina was going through
a pain-free delivery, Gonzalo began to experience pain in
his stomach.

"I have often wondered whether Joseph had pain like this
as he waited for Mary to bring Her only Son into the world
in a stable", he mused. "For if it means I am bearing your
pain, then I am glad of it."

The birth came and went. And while Catalina's health and
strength improved every day, Gonzalo's pain grew worse. He
had hot sweats and fevers, which he did his best to hide.
The last thing he wanted was to cloud her joy in the smallest degree as she looked down at her noisily suckling child.
The fact that Juan grew up short and skinny was not his
mother's fault. Nature, or Providence, could not have been
more bountiful to Catalina in this respect. For nine months
she had so much milk that she was even able to help out a
neighbor by the name of Eulalia. Eulalia gave birth at about
the same time but could not produce much milk of her own.
The "milk brother" of San Juan de la Cruz was very proud
of this title and later professed his vows in the Carmelite
friary of Úbeda as Friar Bartholomew of Good Counsel.

The last two years of Gonzalo's life were filled with joy and
suffering in equal measure. He could not sleep. When he
got up in the morning, he would find he could barely stand.
Pain would shoot down one leg, up the other and straight
into his head. As the day wore on, however, the pain sub-
sided, and he would end up feeling relaxed and pleasantly
surprised at how well he felt. This might have had something to do with a draft that Mother Agueda made from
some berries her brother had sent from a recently discovered country called Peru.

"What marvelous skill these savages have," Gonzalo said, as the sedative effect of the concoction began to work, "if people who have such skill in the easing of pain can be so called."

Catalina watched her husband wasting away before her eyes. But she could not believe he was dying. She put her faith in God and indulged Gonzalo's every whim. If she could just get him to eat, he would surely regain his health. Eusebio did what he could. He was now in his element on the Muñosancho estate. Don Anastasio was utterly dependent on him. He had progressed from Spanish to Latin and was known to the canons of Ávila as Eusebio Latino. (He should not be confused with a Juan Latino, also an Ethiopian slave, who became a professor of grammar at the University of Granada.)

In spite of Eusebio's growing reputation in high circles, he walked the ten miles from Muñosancho to Fontiveros as often as he could. He would always bring a loaf of white bread, or some other delicacy made on the estate, for his old master. By now, however, Gonzalo could keep nothing down but the berry brew. He ate what Eusebio brought, so as not to offend him, but later he would go away and quietly bring it back up. Still, he was glad to see how much his wife and Francisco enjoyed these things. The widow remained stubbornly suspicious of them, however. Her health was also failing and soon after this she died.

But just when they needed him most, Eusebio was pitched onto a course that was to take him toward a preeminence of which no slave could ever have dreamed. Philip II was on the throne of Spain. His father, Charles V, was at war with France over the borders with Spain to the south and the Low Countries to the north. This war was both financially ruinous and costly in terms of human life. In the last year of Gonzalo's life, he said prophetically, "All my life, monarchs have fought over a worthless scrap of land. And the borders of France and Castile have not moved an inch. And I will lay that they will not have done so centuries from now."

History was to prove him right when, not long after this, in 1544 France and Spain signed the Treaty of Crépy. This treaty, on which Eusebio Latino worked as a scribe, negotiated the return of mutual conquests.

Charles V was a good Christian, zealous in his defense of the faith and, apart from the occasional lapse, rigorous in his habits. His zeal precipitated him into a war with the Ottoman Empire that proved as costly as that with France. But he was restrained in victory, choosing not to deal with prisoners in the customary fashion of cutting off hands, hanging or burning at the stake. It was through one of his closest advisers, Fray Antonio de Guevara, who was to become inquisitor of Toledo, that he heard about a "Turk" in Ávila who was fluent in Castilian and Latin. Eusebio was no "Turk", of course. But the term was applied to any dark-skinned person, much as the term "Ethiope" was used to describe any African, whatever country he was from. The emperor and his advisers thought it might be good to have an educated black man on the imperial staff to show that he did not discriminate against people because of their skin color. Black people were by no means unusual in European courts. But they invariably worked as fools or, at best, liveried servants. A black man taking dictation from the imperial secretaries was something quite new.

Antonio de Guevara, a courteous man with a polished and rhetorical literary style, had become acquainted with the grammarian Anastasio Sifuentes, whose work on Nebrija he admired. When Fray Antonio told him he wished to appropriate his slave and give him a job on the imperial staff, the priest replied:

"Give up Eusebio? I would sooner cut off my hands and feet! But, ah me," he added, knowing he had little choice in the matter, "a humble subject must bow to the wishes of his monarch."

Gonzalo was already on his deathbed when Eusebio came to see him to ask his permission, as if they were still master and slave. Gonzalo was surprised that Fray Antonio de Guevara, who had written a book entitled *Menosprecio de corte y alabanza de aldea* (In despite of court and praise of country) should want to take a man like Eusebio from his rural backwater and drop him into the turbulent world of the court.

"I consent," said Gonzalo, "and gladly, on one condition —that you give me your word never to forget what you learned about the ways of God on our journeys, when we would read the Scriptures. I am not long for this world", he went on, sinking back onto his pillow. "We will not meet again in this life. But, my friend, will you give me your word that you will do your best to see to it that we meet in the life to come?"

"With all my heart, master", the African replied with tears in his eyes. "I give you my word to be a good Christian, for after Our Lord Jesus Christ and the Blessed Virgin, there is no one I would rather meet in the hereafter."

This exchange took place in the winter of 1543. Gonzalo died in the spring of the following year. By then Eusebio Latino and his family were with the emperor's entourage in France. Eusebio had had to take a stick to Potenciana to persuade her to go with him. She felt, with some justification, that their life in Muñosancho was about as good as it gets and that she would rather be sitting pretty as a slave than free in some vicious court. It was common knowledge that in itinerant courts servants had no guarantee of being fed.

Right up to the end, Gonzalo would get up and sit for a while in the workshop. He could no longer do much in the way of weaving because of the shaking in his hands. But he found it soothing to sit in the sunshine coming through the windows that he had made with his own hands, listening to the clickety-clack of the loom. One day Catalina said with tears in her eyes:

"How can you be so peaceful? It's almost as if you can't wait to leave us."

"I've had a good life", Gonzalo calmly replied. "For fourteen of my thirty-five years, I've been blessed with a happiness far beyond the dreams of many who live to a ripe old age."

When he could no longer work the loom, he cut a quill and wrote verses. To him it was a blessing to have lived an unenvied and unenvying life, such a quiet life that Don Hernando never heard of him again or carried out his promised vengeance. The modest living this had enabled them to make had brought him perfect contentment.

"What's to become of this little mite, with no father to look up to?" said Catalina reproachfully one day as she nursed baby Juan.

"What could be better for him than what you are now giving him?" he replied. "As for the future, put your trust in Providence. If God has been so generous thus far, why not always?"

Yet Catalina said later that in those last months, the baby, who was less than a year old, grew more and more attached to his father. Though she had carried the baby, given birth to him and nursed him, whenever baby Juan saw Gonzalo he would put his arms up and would not be put down. Juan cried like other babies. But Gonzalo had only to pick him up and he would stop immediately. If Juan would not go to sleep, Gonzalo would cradle him and he would fall blissfully asleep. Some of the neighbors attested to this. At a time when child care was regarded as exclusively the mother's province, this attachment between father and son was remarkable.

Gonzalo was once heard to say, in a semiconscious state, that the child would not have an easy life. Nor would he live as he had done, unenvied and unenvying, but would sometimes be a contradictory symbol, as Our Lord Jesus Christ was. But neither Catalina nor their eldest son Francisco, who were with Gonzalo when he breathed his last, were ever heard to mention this. Nor would they permit such things to be spoken. All they would attest to was the special relationship between Gonzalo and baby Juan and that when Catalina's husband died, her milk suddenly dried up.

Chapter 5

Catalina Alvarez, Widow of a Yepes

Gonzalo's death prostrated Catalina. He died raving, which is not unusual after a long illness, and his last words were not noteworthy.

The fact that Catalina's milk dried up was a serious matter. The baby would not take to anything else, not even donkey's milk, which is the closest to human milk. He simply stopped feeding. He would cry fretfully day and night until he no longer even had the strength to cry. They were convinced Juan would die, watching helplessly as the once-beautiful, well-fed baby turned into a gaunt, hollow-eyed creature. Juan's smallness of stature is probably attributable to this period of his life.

Growing increasingly desperate, Catalina lost her grip on reality. "I am no Job", she exclaimed one day to Mother Agueda, who had remained a close friend of the family. "I have only just lost my husband in his prime. Must I bear the grief of losing my baby as well?"

"This has all the hallmarks of Lucifer", said Mother Agueda, shaking her head.

She was still in possession of all her faculties, and although no longer prioress of the convent of Peñaranda, she had lost none of her considerable moral authority.

"It is not to do with whether the baby lives or dies", she went on. "For he is baptized, and for that reason alone he is surer of Heaven than any of us. It is that such a Christian mother, widow of one of the most exemplary men I ever knew, should so despair as to be in danger of jeopardizing her immortal soul. There are many ways to fight the devil, my child," she continued more gently, "from exorcism to praying to the Blessed Virgin, which is the surest way to defeat him, however often it should prove necessary."

There was a statue of the Virgin in a remote place by the name of Cabizuela that was said to have miraculous powers. It did not take much to persuade Catalina to go on a pilgrimage to Cabizuela with the baby.

They traveled by cart. When the road eventually gave out, they walked the last few miles up a steep, rocky path. Catalina was carrying the exhausted infant in her arms. She would stop every now and then to hold a cup of water from a deep pool to the baby's lips. But it was obvious that the baby was dying, and she wept. Francisco, now thirteen, walked by her side. He had felt the loss of his beloved father deeply—none more so than he. But he had never succumbed to despair or allowed it to shake his faith in God. They were accompanied by Mother Agueda and two devout young sisters from the community.

A hermit, believed by some to be a saint and by others to be mad, lived at the shrine. The man took one look at the baby and declared him to be starving. Then he looked Catalina up and down.

"Woman," he said, "with such endowments as you undoubtedly possess, why can you not feed this child?"

The hermit had received no holy orders. The only reason he was a hermit was that on the whole he preferred living alone. But he was lascivious. He had a reputation for behaving and speaking inappropriately to women.

Mother Agueda knew the man well and rebuked him.

Without a word the hermit withdrew. In the meantime, the pilgrims began to recite the rosary. The hermit soon returned with a toothless woman. Her nut-brown skin was all wrinkled and leathery, like that of a desert nomad.

"She is no Christian", the hermit said. "But not one of her seven children, four of whom still live, ever wanted for milk. For a small recompense she is disposed to give your baby what it seems you cannot."

The two young nuns eyed the woman suspiciously and said they should rely on prayer alone. But Mother Agueda said they might as well see what she could do. Catalina wept as she handed the baby to the woman, who took out a flaccid breast and held it to the baby's parched lips. Fastening on the breast, the baby began to suck, weakly at first but with mounting desperation, until at last he succeeded in getting some milk.

It soon became apparent that Zobeida the Moor, as the woman was known, had a great deal of experience with babies. "Why, the poor little mite has some teeth—look", she began one day with a toothless grin. "We could be feeding him on vetch, Mistress Catalina."

Without another word, she set about making a puree of vetch, a plant well known to poor people and the Moors. At first it gave baby Juan diarrhea, and their hearts sank. But she persevered, mixing the food with flour and sheep's milk. And in the end he accepted it.

On their way back to Peñaranda, the two novices talked incessantly about how the baby had been on the brink of death. They were convinced it had been a miracle. And they had played a part in it with their prayers. Mother Agueda reprimanded them, warning them not to be boastful. They were not to talk of miracles but of Providence. She described what had happened as God working through His creatures to achieve His ends without changing the natural order of things. But privately they continued to call it a miracle. And the story spread that Catalina Alvarez's youngest child had been suckled by the Virgin of Cabizuela herself. This was blasphemy, and the two novices were locked up in punishment cells on bread and water. One of them repented and went on to become an excellent nun. The other left the order and led a dissolute life.

Catalina was kind to Zobeida the Moor, paying her out of what little was left after Gonzalo's funeral. During her fortnight's stay in Cabizuela she kept a watchful eye on the hermit, who made constant advances toward her.

"Mistress Catalina," he began one day, "once your year of mourning is up, will you not think about marrying again? You are young, beautiful even. You ought to have more children. The one we saved is nothing but skin and bone. I would not give much for his chances of survival. There is a farmer . . . a good man. He is no longer in the first flush of youth, but he is not yet in his dotage. And he has a tidy bit of land to work. I have taken the liberty of speaking to him. And he tells me that he is willing to take you and your children in. I do not do this for myself, you understand. God calls me to help in straightening out the affairs of others . . ."

Catalina suspected that in giving such help, there would be something in it for the hermit. But she could not be sure baby Juan's survival had not been a miracle, or whether he had had anything to do with it if so. Fortunately for him, this was enough to prevent her turning him out on his ear. Yet the hermit's words sent a shiver through Catalina. They reminded her, as if she needed reminding, that her situation was precarious.

The widow of La Moraña must have died at around this

time, as there is no further mention of her. Catalina returned to Fontiveros shortly before the outbreak of a famine that gripped Castile for several years. Philip II pegged the price of bread at no lower than eight *reales* a bushel for wheat and half a *ducado* for barley, on pain of banishment and the confiscation of land and goods. He did not believe the land's infertility to be caused by the drought but by the peasants' refusal to work it. But he refused to use one *maravedí* of the wealth that was now pouring in from the New World, scarcely leaving any trace of its passage through Castile on its way to foreign parts, where it was used to finance his numerous wars.

Catalina's savings soon disappeared. When she could no longer pay for her raw materials, the once-busy workshop fell silent. But for the generosity of the nuns of Peñaranda, who barely had enough to feed themselves, she and her children would have starved many times over. And on the advice of Mother Agueda, Catalina reluctantly agreed to seek help from her husband's wealthy family.

"Why should the sins of the father be visited upon the sons?" Mother Agueda pronounced. "Not that it was a sin for Don Gonzalo to spurn his lineage and marry for love. What I mean is, why should the innocent pay? If I were not so old I would come with you to teach those who call themselves Christians a thing or two about the Gospels. But, alas, you see the condition I am in."

The journey to Cabizuela had made Mother Agueda's legs swell up, and she now had to be carried into the choir on a litter. But there was nothing wrong with her mind, and she helped Catalina to think. The Medina branch of the family was still controlled by Don Hernando. So they decided to approach another member of the Yepes family who was not in the silk trade.

There was a priest by the name of Yepes in Torrijos, a district of Toledo. A man of God was sure to be well disposed toward a relative in need. Moreover, he was said to be quite well-off. He was the archdeacon of the collegiate church founded in 1509 by Teresa Enríquez, the first cousin of Ferdinand the Catholic. Also known as "the Madwoman of the Sacrament", she had endowed her hometown of Torrijos with a number of religious and charitable foundations.

Catalina was to look back on this episode as one of the greatest trials of her life. It was only thanks to the generosity of those who took pity on a young woman walking through the mountains with two children, one of them a babe in arms, that she survived the hundred-mile journey.

Later, when times were hard, she was fond of saying: "This is nothing to what we endured on the road to Torrijos. But what was that", she would add, "compared to my joy that Juan was alive when but a few months earlier I had given him up for dead. Yet I had no doubt things would turn out all right in the end, for I knew Gonzalo was in a place from which he was doing all he could to help."

They entered Torrijos through the gate in the Maqueda wall. Catalina gazed in wonder at the splendor of the town with its numerous religious houses, the fertile plain of the river Tagus bending southward. It seemed to her to have escaped the hard times that the rest of Castile was going through.

It was to take five days to get an audience with the archdeacon. During that time, they lodged in a charitable institution established by "the Madwoman of the Sacrament". This was run by sisters known as *sacramentinas*. One of the *sacramentinas* fell for little Juan. Moved by Catalina's plight, she requested an audience with the archdeacon, and at last it was granted.

As soon as Catalina set eyes on the archdeacon, whose full name it would perhaps be best not to mention, her heart sank. He regarded the little family coldly.

"How a young woman", he began at last, "who claims to be related to me could entertain the notion of seeking refuge with her children in the house of a priest is beyond me . . ."

Catalina opened her mouth to speak but he went straight on.

"Leaving aside the deceptions perpetrated by some relatives, still less can I believe that you appear not to know that there are priests whose virtue is not as irreproachable as it should be."

With this he threw them a few coins.

"Now, if you please, be on your way."

Catalina stared at him, too stunned for a moment to react. Then, leaving the coins where they lay, she turned and hurried out with her arm around Francisco.

Catalina sank onto the church steps. Barely able to hold Juan in her arms, she began to sob uncontrollably. Francisco too, normally so stoic, buried his face in his mother's skirts and wept.

A young priest came hurrying out and knelt beside them.

"I was in the church just now", he began a little breathlessly. "I could not help overhearing the archdeacon's words."

The sight of the family, all now weeping on the church steps, clearly distressed the young priest.

"Please," he went on, offering Catalina the handful of coins, "take the money. To refuse it would be an act of pride. You and your children evidently need it."

Looking up into the young priest's eyes, Catalina allowed him to press the coins into her hand.

"There is another Yepes in Galvez, no more than a day's journey from here", he continued. "A physician by the name of Juan de Yepes. He is well known in these parts, not only for his knowledge and skill, but for his kindness. In Galvez I dare say you will find a warmer welcome than you have received here." With this the young priest rose and hurried back into the church.

Juan de Yepes was then in his forties. His wife had remained childless. And though he had never blamed her for it, it had affected her personality. Like any good doctor, he had told her that the fault might just as easily have been his as hers. Catalina and her children were welcomed by the doctor and, at first, by his wife. Gradually, however, she became jealous of the attentions her husband was paying Catalina and she began to make pointed remarks.

"Do you not think", she said one day, "that in your situation the best thing to do is to marry again? You are still young. You need a man to take care of you and your children. With your looks a man should not be too hard to find."

This advice, which was by and large well-meaning, was offered several times. Catalina would listen politely. Then, as on this occasion, she would ignore it.

After the third comment like this, Catalina told the doctor she had decided to return to Fontiveros and get the little workshop going again. He agreed it was probably for the best.

"I will lend you the money to buy the materials you need to start afresh", he said. "Don't worry about paying me back. When you get on your feet again, perhaps . . ."

Catalina thanked him profusely. Waving this aside, he went on:

"I have a proposition. Leave Francisco with me. He's a good boy, and I could do with some help. In payment for his work, I will give him an education. And if he proves diligent and a quick study, I will teach him all I know."

Catalina, who was very close to Francisco, accepted this offer with a heavy heart. Both wept bitterly at their parting.

Catalina's stay in the doctor's house lasted three months. Francisco spent more than a year in Galvez. He was not happy there. The doctor's wife was suffering from depression, which was then known as "melancholy". She took irrational dislikes to people and blamed them for her own troubles. Having taken a dislike to Catalina, she now transferred this to Francisco. He bore it for as long as he could. But when he could take no more, he wrote to his mother, telling her what was going on. As soon as she received the letter, she once again set off from Fontiveros to Galvez.

Francisco took his place in his mother's workshop. He never regretted this, despite having to put up with his mother's occasional disappointment that he had not become a doctor.

"Our Lord also worked with his hands", he once observed. "To me it is an honor to make my way as a weaver. Besides, I do not think God has called me to study books. I learned that in Galvez."

By the time Juan was five he already knew how to read, though nobody had taught him to do so. Catalina believed that God had shared out her husband's gifts between her two sons equally, giving Francisco goodness and Juan knowledge. Francisco loved people so naturally that he was not even aware of it. Juan, on the other hand, was more thoughtful and introspective by nature.

Chapter 6

The Conversion of Francisco de Yepes

The storms of the autumn of 1540 brought to an end the two years of drought that had devastated Castile. What few crops had survived were destroyed by these storms. And with them perished the last hopes of the people who worked the land of the Meseta. Philip II continued to bring in punitive legislation in an attempt to stamp out the huge profits to be made from the starving populace. But there were mutterings that the people would be much better off if, instead of bringing out harsh laws, he were to use some of the gold from the Indies to buy grain from the Dutch. When a band of protestors waylaid a grain convoy from the Low Countries intended for the army, the half-mad priest who led them was hanged in the Plaza Mayor of Toledo.

Some parts of the country were worse hit by famine than others. Fontiveros was among the worst. Set in a completely flat plain of arable land, unbroken by vineyard or vegetable plot, devoid of all industry but the odd weaver's cottage, there was nothing to break the north winds that swept down off the Sierra de Gredos. These icy winds brought black frosts that blighted the crops.

The torrential rains that struck Fontiveros turned the land around the village into a lake, deeper than any in living memory. After two weeks of incessant rain, the murky waters of the lake were teeming with little fish, which the children caught in nets made from rags. Small and bony though these fish were, when the villagers discovered that they were not harmful and could be eaten, they too set about catching them. Their diet had consisted mostly of cabbage and grass, with no protein of any kind, and any addition to the pot was most welcome.

While her two boys fished, Catalina was facing another stark choice. She knew she must leave the workshop once more. It no longer even yielded enough to feed the family on cabbage soup. They must either move away or starve. Arévalo stood between two rivers, the Adaja and the Arevadillo. Its land was comparatively fertile and was not as famine stricken as places less favored by nature. The weaving industry was thriving in Arévalo, and she was confident of finding casual work there. She had a good reputation in the area as a weaver, and Francisco was not far behind.

By now Juan was six. As he sat on the shores of the lake, he pondered a ticklish question. How was it that the water that had fallen from the sky and had seemed quite lifeless had suddenly begun to teem with fish and tadpoles? He would come home and ply his mother and brother with questions about the mystery of life. All they could tell him was that everything sprang from God. He also asked them about infinity, as he strove to grasp the concept of something without end. Not surprisingly it was beyond him, and this troubled him. But he did not spend all his time thinking about things far beyond the scope of a normal six-year-old. He also liked playing with boys of his own age. And when they got tired of catching tadpoles, or when the tadpoles disappeared, they cut ash saplings and tried to spear the darting fish.

One day, as he reached out to retrieve his spear, he fell into the deepest part of the lake. There were no grown-ups about at the time, and Francisco was helping Catalina get ready to move to Arévalo. The other boys were not sure whether this was one of Juan's pranks. When it finally dawned on them that he had been under for a long time, they raised the alarm. A passing shepherd heard their shouts. He listened to their account of what had happened. But seeing no sign of the boy in the water, he feared the worst.

Without much hope, the shepherd began to poke about in the water with his crook. Suddenly a head broke the surface on the far side of the lake. The man ran around to where the boy had surfaced and, catching him around the neck, fished him out onto the bank.

At first the shepherd was angry. He thought the boys had played a trick on him and that Juan had been in on it all along, crouching on the far bank. But when the others crowded around him, demanding to know how he had not drowned when he had been under for so long, the man believed them.

Juan said simply, "A lady held out her hand to me."

Catalina was miserable about having to leave the place where she had been so happy with her husband and sons. She was furious when she heard the story and gave Juan a sound beating for playing dangerous games. But Francisco, who always stood up for his younger brother, said quietly, "Tell me about the lady."

"She was beautiful", Juan replied. "She held her hand out to me. But it was white as snow. And since mine was all muddy, I did not take it."

Years later, when Juan de Yepes had become Fray Juan de la Cruz [Brother John of the Cross], reformer of the Carmelite Order, he would often tell this story. This is surprising, as, for fear of being thought boastful, he was normally reluctant to speak of the special favors conferred on him by the Blessed Virgin.

Shortly before his death, as he journeyed through Andalusia with one of his friars, Fray Martín de la Asunción, they came across a muddy lake of the kind found near the Guadalquivir when the river floods.

"It was in such a lake that Our Lady first appeared to me," he said meditatively, "though I did not know it to be she at the time. And the favor she showed me then has been with me ever since."

Fray Martín adds, "One glimpse of the look in his eye as he gazed at the muddy water was enough to know that he again beheld the Blessed Virgin. This was not strange, for in the last months of his life, if he was not with Our Lord, he was with Our Lady, though he did not allow this to interfere with his sacred duties."

Catalina took a small house on the banks of the Adaja. She occupied one of its two rooms. The brothers shared the other. This also served as the kitchen. Its mean fireplace provided barely enough warmth on cold nights, which seemed to be almost all year round.

Catalina and Francisco found casual work in a weaver's workshop. Juan, meanwhile, went to school. The pittance his mother and brother earned was barely enough to feed the family. After a long day at the loom, they would huddle by the fire and tell stories of the time when Gonzalo was alive. Both boys identified closely with their father. These stories often brought tears to Juan's eyes. It grieved him that he had been too young to have known his father before he died. Francisco, who was now nearly twenty, did his best to take his father's place. He would say: "Your father would have told you to do such and such." And Juan would do it directly.

One day Francisco met a girl from Muriel through a fellow weaver. Her name was Ana Izquierdo. Though poor, she had many good qualities. The emotions she awoke in Francisco transformed him overnight. His attentions toward Ana Izquierdo were by no means improper. It was simply that she stirred longings in him that had lain dormant until then. He thought nothing of walking the nine miles between Arévalo and Muriel to serenade her with his guitar, something that was not unusual at that time. He just wanted to be close to her, even if only through the bars of her window. But he invariably came away feeling frustrated. His friend, Pedro Mellado, was courting a cousin of Ana Izquierdo's, also from Muriel. His intentions, however, were of a somewhat different kind.

"A weaver's life is not so bad", Francisco began one night as they walked home from Muriel.

"What? A lifetime shackled to the loom?" the young man replied. "No, my friend, it's a soldier's life for me. First chance I get, I'm off to the war in Flanders. Or maybe the New World as a conquistador."

"Aren't you going to marry Pepita, then?" Francisco asked, wide-eyed.

"There's only one kind of woman I'll ever marry", Pedro Mellado replied. "One rich enough to pull me out of the pit of poverty into which I had the misfortune to be born."

Francisco told him what he thought of this and of his intentions toward Ana's cousin. But in spite of everything he liked Pedro Mellado. He was good company, and he had some skill with the guitar. They used to stop at an inn on the road from Muriel. And although it was not a respectable place and Pedro Mellado's songs were on the bawdy side, the landlord would pay them a modest sum to sing to the company.

Catalina approved of her son's choice. She had heard good

things about Ana Izquierdo and her family. But the change in her son's behavior troubled her. When summer came, he began to stay out late drinking. She said nothing about it, however. In every other way his behavior was exemplary. No matter how late he came home, he never missed a day's work. He even did what he could to help the family. While Pedro Mellado spent his earnings from the inn, Francisco put bread and other food on the table. He would either buy it or glean it from the fields through which they passed. And then there were the things Ana Izquierdo gave him from her family's small kitchen garden.

One night Francisco came in very late, reeking of wine, his guitar slung on his back. Catalina, who had been waiting up for him, said quietly, "Listen to me, Francisco. You will not dishonor that girl, under any circumstances. Do you understand?"

"Yes mother. I give you my word that I won't."

He was as good as his word. But his behavior did not change. He was young, and he found the temptations he encountered with Pedro Mellado hard to resist. Moreover, Pedro had other equally rowdy friends, and they egged each other on.

One night there was a fiesta dedicated to the August Virgin in a nearby village. After the festivities, they carried on drinking in the fields. They ended up doing a sarabande in the almond orchard of a peasant farmer as the sun came up. Hungry after their exertions, and since the man clearly had more than enough to spare, they helped themselves to his almonds. The almonds were green, however, and tasted bitter. So they destroyed the whole crop. Then they destroyed the vineyard next to the almond orchard for good measure, because the grapes were also unripe.

Juan, who had just turned nine, was waiting for Francisco

to come home. And with a majesty far beyond his nine years, he said, "Brother, do you think our father would have been pleased to see you come in at this hour and in such a condition? Do you think he would have been pleased that you keep our mother up most nights, waiting for you?"

Francisco had been half-expecting something like this. But that it should have come from Juan, that his little brother, normally so deferential to him, had dared to judge him and find fault in his conduct, took him aback.

"From that day," he was later to comment, "our roles were reversed. My little brother became my mentor. The only explanation I can find for the fact that he always knew what to say to guide and comfort the soul was that God had granted him the gift of counsel at an exceptionally early age."

Juan forbade Francisco to say such things in his presence, however. And he insisted that what good there was in him had come from his older brother.

Juan's withering rebuke stopped Francisco in his tracks. He did not even enter the house. Turning on his heel, he went straight to church to confess his misdeed. The priest, Father Carrillo, who was known as a stringent confessor, imposed a heavy penance. He also told Francisco that he must make good the damage he and his friends had done. The first part of his penance, prayers and self-mortification, was to be carried out at the scene of the crime.

Francisco went without food in order to be able to repay the farmer. Whenever he could, he would leave money on the man's doorstep. The farmer, Lepe García, was not surprised to find the money. He knew very well who the culprits were and what the money was for. One day he waited for Francisco and caught him as he was leaving his few coins.

"You'd better do some work on your sums, lad", he said. "The almonds weren't worth that much."

After an awkward silence, he added:

"I hope your mother's well?"

Lepe García was unmarried. For all her troubles, Catalina was still a lively, comparatively young woman, not to mention her reputation in Arévalo as a devoted mother and a skilled weaver. Lepe García was one of her last suitors. He turned out to be a good man. And though it was said that he had vested interests, he helped the family. Whatever his motives, he did not take offense when his advances were gently but firmly rebuffed.

It was at about this time that Francisco began to pick up homeless people from the street. He would bring them back to the house and give them something to eat. Juan marveled at his brother's goodness. Being very fastidious by nature, particularly about personal hygiene, Juan could not overcome his aversion to the filth and the smell of these unfortunate people.

Francisco married Ana Izquierdo in the village of Muriel. Lepe García contributed a kid and three chickens from his farm to the feast. And it was Lepe García who, having accepted his rejection, warned Catalina that hard times were coming to Arévalo. He advised her to move the family to Medina del Campo. Although Medina could also expect hard times, it had become the principal market town of Castile, and one of the most important in Europe. Merchants flocked to Medina from La Mancha, Biscay, Toledo and Córdoba, and even from as far afield as Flanders, France and Portugal. He gave them the name of a wealthy weaver with an establishment on the main street, a man who had no connection with the Yepeses. As it happened, there was no longer anything to fear from Don Hernando. The head of the family was now in his dotage, his memory gone, and he was soon to die.

Catalina once again set off with her family to begin a new life in a new place. All their worldly possessions were loaded onto a small cart. As they could not afford a donkey or mule, they took turns pulling the cart, except for Ana Izquierdo, who was already pregnant. Catalina said she could not have hoped for a better daughter. Ana also became a weaver and was delighted with her new family. And though in time she came to be deeply devoted to Fray Juan de la Cruz, she always maintained that her husband was the saintlier man. No one agreed with her more wholeheartedly than her brother-in-law, who was never so uncomfortable as when miraculous deeds or occurrences were attributed to him.

Something of the kind may have occurred on this journey. A few miles from Medina del Campo, where the meandering river Zapardiel has formed an ox-bow lake, the two brothers saw an apparition. There was not a cloud in the sky. The distant floodplain shimmered in the midday sun. The family had stopped to rest and eat under the trees. While the brothers went to gather more firewood, the women cooked a lentil stew. The brothers suddenly heard a sound behind them, like the rushing of water. At first they took no notice. Francisco was later to describe the event to his confessor, a Carmelite by the name of Juan de San José:

> At first I took it to be the wind. I felt such a shiver run through my body that I thought I must have caught a chill. But though I said nothing at the time, I noticed a change come over my brother's features.

Juan was now nearly eleven years old. In many ways he was just like other boys of his age. But sometimes he would

become thoughtful. And he would ask his brother questions
to which Francisco did not always know the answer.

Overcome by exhaustion, the brothers sank down on the
bank. They said nothing, but kept their eyes fixed on the
lake. As they watched, the water began to rise up in waves,
furling themselves into the shape of a monster, which such
a small lake could not possibly have contained. In his description of the event to Father Juan de San José, Francisco
continues, "It was like a whale in size and form. With its
monstrous jaws agape, it fixed its gaze not upon me but
upon my brother."

Francisco was about to turn and run in terror when he
saw Juan out of the corner of his eye. He was deathly pale
and very still. Francisco placed himself in front of Juan, his
axe at the ready. But, gently lowering Francisco's arm, Juan
calmly made the sign of the Cross. At this the shape disappeared with the same rushing sound.

"Did you see what I saw?" Francisco asked.

"And what was it you saw?" Juan replied after a moment.

"A whale, or something like it."

Whenever the subject of this incident came up, Juan
would tease his brother about the whale. What on earth
had possessed him to say such a thing, he would ask, never
having seen a whale in his life, which was not surprising
since there were no whales in Castile? After he had professed his vows, Juan forbade his brother to mention the incident. But Francisco did not always obey his brother. Neither Catalina nor Ana Izquierdo saw or heard anything of
what had happened at the lake, and the brothers did not
mention it.

But Fray Juan never called his brother a liar or made out
that he was mad. And when years later he wrestled with the
devil in successive exorcisms, he would ask how something

that assumed the shape of a whale in a desert could be taken seriously.

"If it was just an illusion," Francisco asked once when they were talking about the incident, "why did you make the sign of the Cross with such devotion?"

"There is no harm in doing so. Moreover," he added, "if done with thought and feeling, it is like praying with one's body."

Chapter 7

The Orphanage in Medina del Campo

According to the register of the convent of Discalced Carmelites in Medina, Catalina Alvarez took a house in the north of the city. It was one of the poorer houses behind the calle de Santiago, whose stuccoed walls formed part of the house itself. The front consisted of a door and two tiny windows. These let in so little light that by midafternoon and in winter often even earlier, they had to weave by candlelight.

Catalina and Francisco scraped out a living making silk headdresses for the merchant whose name Lepe García had given them. He turned out to be an unreliable employer, however, and they were no better off during that time. Francisco, now head of the family, decided to put Juan into an orphanage. There, if nothing else, he would receive two meals a day.

The orphanage of La Doctrina Cristiana was founded by Don Rodrigo de Dueñas. Don Rodrigo had also endowed the convent of Santa María Magdalena that stood next to it. The reason he gave for undertaking both foundations at once was that while the condition of orphaned boys was tragic, that of young women who had learned so little from their parents that they had turned to prostitution was equally tragic. Hence the convent's dedication to Mary Magdalen, who is said to have been a sinner. The nuns of Santa María Magdalena devoted themselves to the care of fallen women.

The boys of the orphanage were not only taught how to be good Christians, they were also taught a trade. Despite his love of the loom, Francisco knew that his brother would have better prospects if he were to learn a trade with more of a future. He chose carpentry. Houses were then predominantly made of wood, and there was no shortage of building work in Medina del Campo.

As the orphanage itself did not have the facilities to teach trades, its pupils were apprenticed to tradesmen. Juan was sent to a master carpenter from Zaragoza by the name of Pedro Maño, who worked throughout Castile and Aragón. When Juan was nearly fourteen, the age at which apprentices became tradesmen in their own right, Pedro Maño sent the following letter to the orphanage:

> I regret to inform you that I have found Juan de Yepes to lack the strength required to use a saw or plane. Or, if he has the strength, he chooses not to use it. Without this it is not possible to work in the trade of carpentry. I therefore see no point in his continuing in this trade.

The principal of the orphanage, a priest by the name of Don Felix Sangrador, was not an unkind man. But he was of a suspicious nature and was constantly on the lookout for mockery at his expense on the part of the pupils. He was surprised to receive this letter, therefore. For though Juan de Yepes was short and skinny, he was no weakling. He was not exactly brawny, but undoubtedly wiry. One of the duties of the pupils of La Doctrina Cristiana was to attend funerals. To lend solemnity to the occasion, they would process in their coarse woolen cassocks with candles and carrying a standard topped by a heavy metal crucifix. Of all the pupils, Juan was the most tireless standard-bearer. It was so heavy that they had to take turns carrying it. Many of the boys tried to avoid carrying it at all. Yet Juan not only did it willingly, he would scold his fellows for trying to get out of carrying the Holy Cross. Depending on the importance of the deceased and the solemnity of the funeral, the orphans would receive payment known as "candle alms" for this work, which went toward the upkeep of the orphanage.

When Don Felix received Pedro Maño's letter, he concluded that Juan had either been lazy or negligent in his apprenticeship. After putting Juan on bread and water for three days, he sent him to a master house painter. Juan did no better at this. The paint fumes made him dizzy, and instead of painting walls he spent his time painting figures. Don Felix decided there was little more the orphanage could do for him, and he was sent home.

Many years later, at the time of the beatification of Fray Juan de la Cruz, an old Augustinian nun who had been a novice in the convent of Santa María Magdalena made the following deposition:

> Fray Juan de la Cruz was then a boy of fourteen or so. He lived next door to us in the orphanage of La Doctrina Cristiana. He was there to receive instruction in the faith and learn a trade by which he might earn his living. In the latter at least, not surprisingly, in view of the greatness to which he was called, he did not succeed. He must already have known that he was being called and that a trade was not for him. In spite of this he always professed a sense of shame at not having become a carpenter, like Our Lord Jesus Christ. But God had other ideas for him, and he did not get on either as a carpenter or as a house painter. Only later did his skill as a painter manifest itself. His brother, Francisco, who was no less saintly than he, is also said to have urged him to try his hand as a tailor and as an engraver, since going home was out of the question—not for want of love but because of the hardship of those times, which were exceedingly hard for all Castile.
>
> He was on the point of leaving the orphanage when our

reverend mother the prioress intervened. From her first meeting with him, she discerned a quality of exceptional devotion in him that she had no intention of allowing to go to waste. Not long after his admission to the orphanage, we heard that Juan de Yepes had gotten on the wrong side of an older boy. It seems the boy accused Fray Juan of being obsequious to the nuns, an accusation that, as we shall see, was false. One day, as they walked in the grounds of the orphanage near a deep well, which was full almost to the brim, the boy threw him in. And with a sneer, the boy bade him ask the Virgin to get him out. He said this because of the veneration in which our devout Fray Juan held the Blessed Virgin Mary, this having annoyed the malevolent boy still further.

That he did not drown in the well is known. But our reverend mother the prioress told us to ignore this, for who can say whether he escaped by his own efforts or with the help of the Blessed Virgin? She bade us rather mark his disposition toward all that touched on the service of God. Our church stood next door to the orphanage of La Doctrina Cristiana. Every day, by order of Don Rodrigo de Dueñas, four of its pupils would act as altar boys at our offices and clean the sacristy and other parts of the church under the supervision of the chaplain and our prioress. In summer they performed these duties between six and ten in the morning and between seven and eleven in winter. After midday, unless required by the chaplain or mother superior for some other purpose, they were free. Some would perform their duties slackly or sullenly, forever endeavoring to cut their hours and scheming how to get hold of the unconsecrated wafers and even the altar wine. Others performed their duties more diligently. Juan de Yepes was among these.

We did not pay them for these services in food or clothing. This fell to our benefactor, Don Rodrigo de Dueñas. In spite of this, our mother superior used to give out little tidbits from our pastry larder. These pastries were sold, at

the door that opens onto the calle de las Animas, to those
who were disposed to be charitable to us. It must be said
that these cakes and pastries were exceedingly delicious and
much sought after by the people of the neighborhood. As
I say, our prioress used to give these delicacies (or more
precisely the scraps, which could not be wrapped and sold)
to the altar boys as rewards. They were not given to every
boy, however, but to each according to his merit. Thus it fell
out that Juan de Yepes was especially favored in this regard.
The gravity of his bearing as he moved about the church
and sacristy was beyond imagination. He was like an angel.
It was this quality that our prioress bade us mark and not be
forever wondering whether the Blessed Virgin had helped
him get out of the well or not.

The sacristy was a small, low-ceilinged chamber with two
narrow windows. In winter especially, the draft these windows let in was such that the altar boys would do anything
to get out of their duties there, preferring to go out into
a sheltered and sunny alley to play at ball. Juan de Yepes
was not above joining in these games, and not without some
skill. But he would do so only if there was no service at the
time. In that case, he would sit quietly in the sacristy and
endure the bitter cold. The church, for all its beauty, with
its Latin cross and arris vaulting decorated with roses, shells
and gilded florets, is every bit as cold as the sacristy. Yet Juan
de Yepes would stand for hours, as if in a trance, gazing at
the paintings on the high altar, allegorical representations
and scenes from the Scriptures. It was when he was in this
state that the prioress bade us mark his devotion. This we
would do through the choir railings. It is also worthy of note
that we did not need to keep an eye on him when he went
into places set apart for Our Lord, such as the sanctuary.
There he would fall to his knees and gaze upon Him in rapt
stillness, his lips moving silently, as though discoursing with
Him. And there was another thing. If the chaplain had any
cause to reprimand Juan de Yepes, it was that during Mass, at

the Consecration, he was so transfixed that he often forgot to ring the bell. It was for these reasons that he was singled out by the prioress, and by us to an extent. And I believe it was this quality that gave rise to the enmity of the fellow who threw him into the well.

Juan de Yepes was a model of obedience, fulfilling his obligations to his superiors in every respect but one. The convent was a refuge for fallen women and others who were not beyond redemption, but all of whom had fallen prey to the same evil, that of prostitution. Or should I say of want? For most had found themselves in that trade not out of lasciviousness but out of poverty. Some were very young and would have been glad to throw off the fetters of this evil. Others were more steeped in depravity, especially if they had already succumbed to the pox and believed themselves lost. With the former we were able to do something. And once set on the right road, we endeavored to find them work, or husbands. This we did by sending them out to the Indies, where they were not so set apart, for being white and Christian, they were preferred by many of the settlers (though not all, by any means) to the native women. In time some of these women became wealthy. And upon their return they were sometimes exceedingly liberal with their money, not only to repay us for what we had done for them, but to help us in our work with others of their kind. Some were content merely to be good wives, for a woman who has had to endure the ignomy of selling her body is likely to find almost anything else preferable, even if only to be the wife of a man of base character.

For those with the pox, it was another kettle of fish altogether. It is well known that this disease was brought by soldiers who had been fighting in foreign parts, the Low Countries and other heretical lands for the most part. So widespread was it that at the time there were fourteen hospitals in Medina del Campo alone. Most of these were dedicated to the treatment of this pestilence and other no less contagious diseases. One of these hospitals, as they are now called, that of Our Lady of the Immaculate Conception, properly known as the Hospital for Venereal Diseases, was divided into two wards, one for men and one for women. It was situated in the *Barrionueva* [the New Town] between the Convent of Our Lady of Grace and the Jesuit college. And when we could do no more for our "fallen women", it was to that place that we sent them.

The question of what to do about these women vexed our superiors. In the end my lord bishop had to intervene. As I say, our convent stood next to the orphanage of La Doctrina Cristiana, some of whose pupils were sixteen or older. Little wonder, therefore, that a number of the boys should endeavor to become acquainted with these women, whether out of simple curiosity, or with less innocent intentions. And though we did our best to keep them apart and prevent all society between them, we did not always succeed in this and had several troublesome incidents. It was only when our benefactor, Don Rodrigo de Dueñas, ordered the building of a separate house for the orphans, that of La Doctrina Cristiana, with its own endowment, that this vexatious problem was remedied. And "with the snuffing of the candle, the moths disappeared", as they say. But until the new house was finished, the only thing to do was to forbid the boys to go near the refuge for "fallen women", upon a strict injunction of expulsion from the orphanage if wrongful intent were proved.

One day our reverend mother prioress received word that Juan de Yepes had been flouting the injunction. It seemed he had been slipping out of the sacristy by the side door into the alley leading to the refuge, in order to visit one of its inmates. The woman in question was yet young. She was the wife of a soldier who had gone to the wars in Italy, leaving her and their little daughter to fend for themselves. As a result, she had become a prostitute. Whether this was out of a need to care for the child or because of a hatred

for men, I cannot say. The fact remains that she continued
to consort with men after contracting the pox, little caring
what harm she did thereby. We had resolved to send her to
the Hospital for Venereal Diseases. But she vowed to take
her own life if we did, which made us think again. The
woman was inconsolable, her daughter having died in early
infancy, which had turned her wits. Her husband too was
killed at Messina, at which she was said to have rejoiced. But
it was not so, for those who knew her testified that while he
was still alive she had had hopes of his return one day, and
this had caused her to moderate her conduct. The truth is,
we did not know what to do with her. It was at this point
that we heard Juan de Yepes had been visiting her. He was
now among the oldest in the orphanage, being sixteen or
so, and it was by no means unheard of for a mature woman
to ensnare a boy on the brink of manhood. In spite of her
infirmity, the woman was comely, her complexion smooth,
the sores or buboes proper to her malady being in hidden
parts of her body.

Had it been any other boy, no pretext or excuse would
have availed him. The matter would have been referred to
Don Felix Sangrador, who would have thrown him out upon
the instant, as he had done to others before. Nor would Don
Felix have been unduly troubled in so doing, despite being
among those who believed Juan de Yepes to be more suited
to a religious life than to the learning of a trade. But our
prioress was convinced of his innocence and made us vow
not to say anything about the matter until we had gotten
to the bottom of it. We set a watch. And the first thing we
discovered was that the report about the secret visits was
true. Juan de Yepes was indeed going to Ana Tordesillas, to
give the woman her proper name, and giving her the pastries
he had earned for good conduct. And for these she was exceedingly grateful, for the pox causes great discomfort, not
to say pain. In her case this was attended by a raging thirst, a
revulsion for certain foods and a craving for others. It seems

Ana Tordesillas had conceived a craving for sweet things, for she believed that by eating sweetmeats and drinking a lot of water thereafter, she could purge her body of its ills.

The sister sacristan, who had brought the matter to our attention, scoffed at this. She said all such cases started out thus and that Juan de Yepes was only giving the woman his pastries to get into her good books in order to obtain greater favors. But there were others among us who believed his motives to be charitable, even if he was misguided in his method. Our discourse on the matter had reached this point when our mother superior resolved to summon his elder brother Francisco to acquaint him with what had happened.

"My brother visiting a person with an infectious disease?" he exclaimed with incredulity.

And he went on to explain what was already common knowledge in Medina—that for his part, he had resolved not to pass by any destitute person. This devotion, which had started in Fontiveros and Arévalo, had reached such a point that if he came upon someone who was too weak or infirm to walk, he would pick the unfortunate person up and carry him to the hospital on his shoulders. And in this, he assured us, he had the help and approval of both his mother and his wife. But not that of his brother Juan. His brother, he confided, was so fastidious in matters of bodily cleanliness that he could not bring himself to touch the poor in all their wretchedness and filth, particularly if their ailment might be contagious. Hence Francisco's disbelief that his brother was supposed to be frequenting such a person, who was also infectious. But still less could he be persuaded that there was any base motive in his attentions toward Ana Tordesillas. For he believed his brother to be the saintliest of men and that Our Lord and the Blessed Virgin had conferred special favors on him from an early age. The sole exception was this abhorrence of the poor, which Juan endeavored to conceal, though he did not always succeed in this.

What happened next was a marvel. I will not go so far as to call it a miracle, but it was a great blessing for many people. With the consent of Francisco de Yepes, we went to the chaplain of the convent and asked him to speak to the offender. We desired him to tell Juan de Yepes that he was discovered and demand what he had to say about the matter. What he said was this: that he was very sensible of his failing in the eyes of Our Lord, who never shrank from the touch of lepers—this, he said, was what had prompted him in the first instance to visit this fallen woman; that he had subsequently been moved to compassion, the pastries he had given her seeming to dispel a measure of the despair that, he believed, would have been the end of her; that he had given her words of consolation and spoken to her of Our Lord's suffering for mankind; and that the woman had received these things gladly.

The blessing lay in that the chaplain was also chaplain of the Hospital of Our Lady of the Immaculate Conception, the Hospital for Venereal Diseases. This hospital was owned by an eminent nobleman, Alonso Alvarez de Toledo, who had withdrawn from the world and was now living an enclosed life in the hospital in order to look after the poor and the sick. The chaplain was so moved by Juan de Yepes' confession that he told Don Alonso of it.

"What I could do with a young man like that by my side in the hospital!" Don Alonso had exclaimed.

It wanted little to satisfy him in this, for no sooner had Juan de Yepes heard of it than he readily consented to leave the orphanage in which he had already stayed overlong. He duly took up his place as a nurse in the Hospital of Our Lady of the Immaculate Conception, giving many thanks to God that with all his squeamishness about the sick and the poor, he should end up being their servant. And with him went Ana Tordesillas. I do not say she accompanied him. But knowing the only person who had succeeded in consoling her to be there, she had no hesitation in consenting to be admitted to the Hospital for Venereal Diseases. And there she was cured, this in turn enabling her to marry a conquistador from the island of Hispaniola, God be praised.

So it was that the disobedience of Juan de Yepes in his youth led to some good, not only for Ana Tordesillas but for many others who were cured at the skillful hands of so excellent a nurse. Don Alonso soon realized that Juan was destined for greater things, however, and gave him leave to study every day, without deduction from his wages, at the Jesuit college a short distance from the hospital. Although the college had been founded by the Jesuit fathers in 1551 for scholars, able pupils from humbler origins were also admitted. Juan de Yepes was one of these. He admired the teachers of the college, none other than Father Capella and Father Astete, who wrote the catechism that we use to this day. He could not have had better teachers, nor did he lag far behind them as a pupil.

Don Alonso's thinking in giving Juan leave to pursue this and more besides was this: that on completion of his studies at the Jesuit college, Juan would seek ordination. Don Alonso would then offer him the chaplaincy of the hospital, which he fervently hoped Juan would accept. It was our belief, however, that things would turn out differently, for the Jesuit fathers had already singled him out as one to keep for themselves. In the end he did neither, for when he came out he took the brown habit and white cowl of Carmel. Such is the Lord's way. When Fray Juan left the Jesuit college and took the Carmelite habit, he was twenty-one years old and had already won wide renown as a Latin scholar and rhetorician.

Chapter 8

The Vocation of
Fray Juan de Santo Matía

On his way to his final retirement in Yuste, the emperor
Charles V stopped in Medina del Campo. Here he stayed
in the palace of Don Rodrigo de Dueñas, founder of La
Doctrina Cristiana. Don Rodrigo's palace, an exceptionally
fine stone and brick house with a tower of homage and a
Renaissance central courtyard, stood on the calle de Santiago, near the convent of La Magdalena.

As befitted a man who was about to retire from worldly
affairs, the emperor had a small retinue, consisting of a
handful of soldiers and men of letters. Among these was
the Ethiopian Eusebio, formerly Gonzalo de Yepes' slave,
who had now risen to the august position of amanuensis to
the emperor's principal private secretary. "Amanuensis" is
something of a misnomer, as he had proved to be such an
accomplished linguist that all court records were written by
him, whether in Latin, Italian, French or Flemish.

Eusebio Latino scoured Medina for the Yepes family,
whom he had not forgotten. But he sent his letters to
Fontiveros, thinking that they would still be living there,
working in his old master's beloved workshop. As a result,
the letters went astray. The Yepes family was no longer what
it had been under Don Hernando, who was dead. It was
from servants of his eldest daughter that Eusebio learned

the whereabouts of Catalina Alvarez. As it happened, she was living close by in the parish of Santiago. Their meeting was charged with emotion. On the one hand, Catalina said she owed all her happiness to the African, who had urged his master Gonzalo to be guided by the noblest prompting of his heart and marry the ward of the widow of La Moraña. The African, meanwhile, enumerated the seemingly endless things Gonzalo had done for him.

"But of the many things he did for me," he said, "none was so great as to treat me as his friend. I have never forgotten the occasion on which he dismounted so that I might ride for a while on the horse. If I were to buy you the best house in Medina, it would not go even halfway to repaying you for this deed alone. But alas, I cannot afford such a thing, nor a fraction of it, for Don Gonzalo taught me to esteem honor above wealth, and so I do. But above all he wanted me to be a good Christian. And on this I gave him my word when I saw him for the last time, as he lay dying. And not for anything in this world would I forgo the joy of meeting him in the next. I have no money, but if there is any other way in which I can be of service to you, you have but to name it."

Catalina and Francisco said that to hear him speak about Gonzalo in these terms was more than enough. The African persisted, however, and at last Francisco admitted that the amount of work coming into the workshop could easily be done by his mother and his wife and that he had been trying to find a position in a large house but without success. It did not take Eusebio long to spread the word among the people visiting the palace where the emperor was staying. A few days later, Francisco was taken on as a squire by two noblewomen living on the calle de Santiago.

During the Emperor's two-week stay in Medina, Eusebio

visited Catalina every day. As soon as he heard about Juan and his growing reputation, Eusebio went to see him at the Jesuit college.

"Although he bears little or no resemblance to Master Gonzalo," Eusebio declared after their first meeting, "I would have known him to be his son anywhere. He has something of his father's serenity, and there is a telltale softness about his eye. But it is in his words, which have the stamp of sincerity, that he is the very image of his father. He longed to know about Master Gonzalo, the man his father had been, his character, the things he had thought about when we were friends. When I told him that he was more like a father to me than a friend, he said he envied me this above all. What most surprised me, however, was that it seems he has resolved not to marry. I asked him why. He replied that it was because he could never be as good a husband and father as his father was."

Catalina also looked surprised at this. But Francisco nodded. In one of his conversations with his brother on this subject, Francisco exclaimed: "Marry? Why brother, were you not born to be a friar?"

"No," the saint replied, "no one is born anything. There are only two exceptions, which are predetermined by God. The first is our sex. We are born either male or female. This is in itself a singular act of selection from among the numberless souls our Heavenly Father holds in His mind. The only reason why we were chosen to come into the world from among so many is that He expects each and every one of us to do something no one else can do better. The second is the religion into which we are born. To be born Christian is a great honor. There is none greater. And it is one of which we are unworthy, particularly at our baptism, when we have not yet reached the age at which we can reason.

From that point on, it is up to us to choose which path to follow. The Lord may hint in His way which path is best. But the choice of whether to accept or reject it is ours and ours alone."

"And yet", Francisco replied, "it was obvious to me from the very beginning that you would be a friar one day. I never once saw you show any interest in a girl, even a virtuous one. Whenever we were in the presence of a woman, except our mother, of course, you always averted your eyes."

"Not averted," Juan replied, "held in check. For if I had loosed them, who can say where it might have led?"

Fray Juan was to deal with the question of the eyes at great length, reminding his friars that they were flesh and blood and that flesh attracts flesh unless tempered by the soul.

"Even as a boy," he continued, "I knew the Lord was calling me to a religious life and that no other life would do. But I resisted it for a long time because my life in the world was so attractive, an ordered life, like your own and our father's, with a wife and children beside you."

"Why did you reject it, then?" Francisco asked, though he knew the answer.

"Because the Holy Spirit made it clear to me in a thousand ways that this was not the path the Lord wanted me to follow. But when I say that a religious life is the only life I could have led, I say it with all the humility of which I am capable. For it seems to me that, having made the decision to give my life to God, a life in a monastery would be no great hardship, whereas a life as a husband and father would be a tough choice. I have the highest respect for those who take this path and regard them as far greater saints than those who lead cloistered lives in a monastery or convent."

"No great hardship? What about the scourge? Haven't

you often been accused of excessive mortification of the flesh?"

"As to that, it must be so", Juan replied simply. "For the flesh is weak and very hard to control. More than this I cannot say."

When Francisco entered the service of the two noblewomen, Juan was in his last year at the Hospital for Venereal Diseases. The two brothers used to see a good deal of one another, as Francisco came across many sick people on the streets. But after taking up his new position, they seldom met. The ladies were not too keen on their servant picking up beggars on the streets of Medina. He attended the ladies in a doublet, emblazoned with their coat of arms, and a sword. He was to keep at a respectful distance at all times and see to it that the carriage was punctual. When they took the coach, he was supposed to sit beside the coachman and shout at the people in the street to make way, maintaining an air of dignity if possible. He occasionally met his brother in the course of these duties. Juan would be going from house to house soliciting alms for the hospital. One day Juan saw Francisco waiting outside the door of the Church of Santiago, where his mistresses had gone to hear Mass.

"Brother, what are you doing out here?" said Juan in surprise. "Why are you not inside?"

"I am commanded to wait outside", Francisco replied.

"Then it is a poor command. For not only do you stand idle at Our Lord's door, it means you are not doing God's work with the sick and needy. I ask you, brother, in all honesty, do you think a man in his thirties should be going about in the apparel of war yet not going to war? Should you be a servant of ladies whose concern for appearances is matched only by their lack of concern for others? Has our family ever wanted for a crust of bread? No. Nor shall it, if we do God's work."

No sooner had Juan said these words than Francisco strode into the church. Under the astonished gaze of the two ladies and the rest of the congregation, he threw himself down at the foot of the sanctuary steps and begged forgiveness for his mistake. Then he left the church and went home. A day or two later, a quartermaster sent by Eusebio Latino came to the family workshop and placed such a large order that they had to take on two extra weavers. It did not make them rich. But from that day on they were able to provide for their basic needs and even moved to a bigger house near the main square.

This incident only increased Francisco's respect for his younger brother, and he attributed him with the gifts of counsel and speaking unerringly. Juan refuted this, however. He said speaking unerringly was a divine attribute and could be claimed by no mortal, not even the prophets. And he gave him examples from the Old Testament of prophets who spoke in error. This did not stop Francisco seeking his brother's advice. But Juan never wanted to be his confessor or spiritual director. This was initially undertaken by a Jesuit and then by a Carmelite by the name of Fray José de Velasco. Francisco made a deep impression on Father Velasco, and he asked his penitent to write an account of his life. As Francisco was already an old man with failing sight by then, Father Velasco appointed three secretaries to help him. This prompted speculation that Francisco was illiterate. Others, however, held that while his literary skill fell somewhat short of his brother's, he had enough for the task, if not quite enough for a full autobiography. It is also clear that although the original request was to write about his own life, he ended up writing about his brother's. Needless to say, Father Velasco, himself a Discalced Carmelite and a devout follower of one of the Order's founders, did not object.

Two of the three secretaries appointed by Father Velasco, Antonio de Santiago and Tomás Pérez de Molina, were from Medina. The third, Francisco de la Peña, was a Franciscan professor. Father Velasco edited the several strands of this account and published it in Valladolid in 1617 under the title *Life and virtues of the Venerable Francisco de Yepes, who died in Medina del Campo in the year 1607: Containing many things of note about the life and miraculous works of his saintly brother, Father John of the Cross.*

The soul, it seems, is as susceptible to maladies that end in madness as the body is to epidemics like the plague. Something of the kind was happening in Castile at about that time. For to bring a child into the world, only to leave it in the doorway of a church at the mercy of the elements, is little short of madness.

This problem was particularly prevalent in Medina del Campo. The finger of blame was pointed at the many merchants who came from all over Europe, and the young women who were drawn to them. Many of these were seduced with false promises of marriage and did not know what to do with the inevitable consequence. The merchants of the Low Countries were among the worst offenders. A young woman's virtue was so little prized in that part of the world that a stain on her honor was considered no dishonor. In Castile it was not uncommon for girls from humble families to earn the money they needed for their dowries in a brothel. If they became pregnant, they would deal with it in the old-fashioned way of going to a back-street crone. Some of these were Moorish women who must have turned from their religion, Islam being as staunch as Christianity in its condemnation of abortion. In Islamic countries, women who broke the religious laws were burned at the stake.

A remarkable series of entries recording the baptism of foundlings left at the church door appears in the register of the Church of Santiago in Medina, the biggest church in the city. As Catalina walked through the streets of Medina one spring morning in 1563, she found a baby left in the doorway of the Church of San Martín. She knew at a glance that the baby was near death. She shouted at the top of her voice to be let in, so that it could be baptized without delay. But the doors remained shut. She picked the baby up and ran to the Hospital for Venereal Diseases, where Juan worked. Juan asked the chaplain, Don Juan Flores, to baptize the child and named Catalina and himself as its adoptive parents. Catalina took the baby home and cared for it lovingly with the help of Ana Izquierdo. Then one day, just when she had begun to think the baby might survive, she found it lying dead in its crib. The loss affected her as if it had been her own child.

"Do not weep so, Mother", Juan said gently. "Admirable though your grief is, you did all you could. Most importantly, you made sure it was baptized. And in so doing you laid it at the gates of Heaven itself. Besides, it is a sign. We must now do the same for as many babies like this as we can find."

This was all it required to make the family spring into action. For all his self-deprecating manner, they hung on his words. Francisco de Yepes became famous throughout Medina and the region in those years. He would rise before dawn and go around to all the churches in the city looking for abandoned babies. He would immediately arrange for them to be baptized and tried to find wet nurses willing to take them, either out of charity or for money. For this he needed financial support.

Francisco disliked begging. But when Juan explained that he was doing the person whom he was entreating a favor, he reluctantly agreed.

"What about the two ladies you served?" Juan said one day.

"Are you mad?" Francisco retorted. "Have you any idea how angry they were when I walked out? As for getting anything out of them, you can forget it. Why, they hang on to their purses as if their lives depend on not spending a single *maravedí*, if they can avoid it."

"And do you mean to let them go to their graves with the weight of all that money pressing down on them?" Juan returned. "Do you not think that on Judgment Day, they will call you to account for not opening their eyes in such an important matter?"

Francisco was not persuaded by this. Nor by several further attempts made by Juan. But he went in the end. And in his account to Father Velasco he described it as something of a miracle. For the ladies not only opened their purses, they persuaded other wealthy people in the city to help. Moreover, both ladies, Doña Concepción Solana and Doña Juana Portilla, appear in the baptismal registers of the Churches of Santiago and San Martín as adoptive mothers of foundlings.

But by far the most entries are those in which the adoptive parents were Francisco de Yepes, Juan de Yepes, Catalina Alvarez and Ana Izquierdo. Indeed, Juan was so committed to this project for foundlings that it was rumored he was about to profess his vows in the order of the hospital of a madman by the name of Juan de Dios, who roamed the streets shouting at the top of his voice. The man took care of the old, the poor, the orphaned and the wretched. Of these, foundlings were considered the most wretched, as their parents were unknown.

To everyone's surprise, however, Juan had other plans. In the spring of 1563, after graduating with distinction in all four humanities courses at the Jesuit college, keenly pursued by the Jesuits, Dominicans, Benedictines, Franciscans and Augustinians, he went secretly to the friary of Santa Ana to ask if he could take the habit of Our Lady of Mount Carmel. No one was more surprised than the prior, Fray Ildefonso Ruiz. Not only had he never met Juan de Yepes, he knew no more about him than what was already common knowledge—his exceptional ability as a Latin scholar and rhetorician.

"What brings you to our door?" the prior inquired.

"The Blessed Virgin", Juan replied.

The small Carmelite community lived in a tiny house next to the Church of Santa Ana in the southwest of the city. Its dozen or so elderly friars met to discuss the question of his joining them. Their response was guarded. With kindly concern on the part of some, and envy on the part of others, they informed him that though the Scriptures were revered in that house, they were not studied as closely as in other houses. Was he quite sure he knew what he was doing? The last thing any of them wanted was that he should regret squandering his God-given talent for the study of the humanities.

"The only talent I know beyond doubt I possess", he replied, "is my love for the Blessed Virgin, to whom I gave my life at a very early age. If she is especially venerated by the Carmelites, then a Carmelite I will be, if you will have me."

"Ah," said an old friar by the name of Fray Bernardo de Cantueso, "if Our Lady is involved, there is little point in further discussion."

Thus, to the dismay of all who knew him, as the Carmelite Order was in chaos at the time, he took the brown and white habit under the name of Fray Juan de Santo Matía (Brother John of Saint Matthias). The Order was split by so many disputes between provinces that in 1530 Charles V had instructed the father general, Fray Nicolás Audet, to reform the provinces of Castile and Andalusia. Failure to do this would leave him no choice but to order their dissolution. The emperor issued this threat because the decadence that ran like a cancer through the once-glorious Carmelite Order—and the resulting strife between rival factions—was the scandal of the Christian world. One contemporaneous historian wrote: "There remain but six monasteries in Castile, and they are all but deserted."

In his account to Father Velasco, Francisco de Yepes alludes to his brother's joining the Carmelite Order as follows:

> His decision troubled us more than we could say. We could not understand why, when he was wanted by so many orders, he should have chosen to enter one in which he was wanted by so few, if any. I confess it made me weep, for it had been my fervent hope that my brother would become chaplain of the Hospital for Venereal Diseases. Had he done so, I would have spent the rest of my life working by his side, helping him with the sick and needy, a thing that was close to both our hearts. One day our mother took me to task for saying that no one wanted him in Carmel. "Is not the Blessed Virgin Mary someone?" she asked. For she knew that he had owed his life to her since the day she plucked

him from the lake in Fontiveros, maybe even since the day he was laid half-dead at the feet of the Virgin of Cabizuela.

It has been said that his sole intention in joining the Carmelite Order, the least rigorous of all the orders at the time, was to reform it. This was not so. It never entered his head to do such a thing until he met Mother Teresa of Jesus. It was she who encouraged him in this. Naturally, I visited him in the tiny friary of Santa Ana, where all he wanted was to be left alone, spending long hours in prayer. Such spare time as he had he spent composing little verses in the pastoral style, in which he thanked Our Lord for enabling him to enter a religious life by the grace of His Holy Mother. This I know for certain, for whenever he finished one of these verses he would entreat me to accompany him on the flute, so that for us they became like little prayers.

The proof that he did not join the Carmelite Order to reform it is that after four years, having failed to find in it the withdrawal from the world he sought, he resolved to become a Carthusian. And but for his chance encounter with Mother Teresa of Jesus, as already mentioned, he would have done so.

He met La Madre two or three years after he began at the Carmelite college in Salamanca in 1565, and from which he benefited greatly. Small wonder, seeing that one of his teachers there was Fray Luis de León.

Chapter 9

John of the Cross

Mother Teresa, or "La Madre" as she was often known, came to Medina del Campo on August 14, 1567, to found her second convent for Discalced Carmelite nuns.

Teresa's school days were fraught with difficulty, largely because of her fiery temperament. Just when it seemed likely she would not be entering the religious life, she was called to one. At first she was reluctant to accept the call. Then one day she came face to face with a figure of Christ on the Cross. The experience had such a devastating effect on her that from that day she became His faithful bride. After professing her vows in the Carmelite Order, she settled down to the life of a quiet, devout nun in the convent of La Encarnación in Ávila. One day she had a vision of hell that frightened her so much that she resolved from then on to observe the rule of the Order as closely as she could. She believed that in order to do so she must get as close as possible to the life led by the first fathers who lived on Mount Carmel, a life of complete simplicity and poverty.

Teresa de Jesús was a firm believer in the power of prayer. She believed that through prayer many souls could be saved from damnation and that prayer could even sway the minds of kings and potentates to rule with greater compassion. But to be most effective, it must take place under rigorous conditions. The heart must be stripped of all yearning for anything but God. And she believed this was impossible in the context of a comfortable, if not decadent, lifestyle. It was this that prompted her longing for the rigor of the life the founding fathers of Carmel had led. Such a life had little or nothing in common with the antics of the nuns of La Encarnación, who traipsed in and out of each other's cells with messages, notes and even love letters and small gifts, all of which were damaging to the soul.

One afternoon in the autumn of 1560 she came to a decision. She must found houses of her own, which would be more like hermitages than convents. In these houses, as far as possible, the poverty of the ancient Carmelites would be re-created. She had great difficulty obtaining the necessary permission from the provincial of the Order. But as it was God's work she was doing, in the end, she succeeded. And on August 24, 1562, she founded the convent of San José in Ávila, the first Discalced, or "barefoot", Carmelite house. In the spring of 1567 the principal general of the Order, Fray Juan Bautista Rubeo de Rávena, passed through Ávila. He was so struck by the piety that reigned in this house that he authorized Mother Teresa to found "as many houses like it as she had hairs on her head". He also gave her permission to found two contemplative houses for reformed friars of the same Discalced Order. She needed this because her nuns must have confessors who shared their beliefs, not those to whom their lives would seem excessively rigorous.

Not surprisingly, it proved more difficult than she had anticipated to find friars who were willing to live and work under the authority of women. The first to offer himself was the Carmelite prior of Medina del Campo, Fray Antonio de Heredia. Mother Teresa rejected him, however, because he was already over sixty. Before Medina, he had held the priorates of Requena, Toledo and Ávila. She doubted his ability to accept the severity of the new rule, as he was more accustomed to giving orders than to taking them. That he was an impressive-looking man, an excellent speaker, and proud, perhaps a little too preoccupied with the whiteness of his habit, also counted against him.

Fray Antonio de Heredia encouraged Mother Teresa to found the second reformed convent in Medina del Campo. Indeed, he bought her a house for the purpose. On the day of the inauguration, he went to Arévalo to meet her and her nuns. He also provided them with all they needed for the altar. Despite all this, Mother Teresa still would not accept him. She wanted the first Discalced friars to be young men.

Francisco alludes to this in his account as follows:

> With all due respect to the memory of La Madre, I cannot but be amused by how mistaken she was in the matter of the much-venerated Fray Antonio de Heredia. Once, in Duruelo, I heard her discoursing on the subject of his age with my own ears. Yet it turned out he lived into his nineties. Indeed, he outlived not only my brother, the Revered Fray Juan de la Cruz, but Mother Teresa herself. Fray Antonio died in the odor of sanctity in Vélez, near Málaga, in 1601, some four years since. He was of great service to the Reform of the Order, holding several prelacies. And despite his great age, he was the provincial of several provinces. When their time came, he helped both La Madre and Fray Juan at the hour of their death. And as their superior, he celebrated their obsequies. From this we may infer that the gift of prophecy is not given to all saints, for in this La Madre was quite mistaken.

Mother Teresa was already in her fifties when she met Fray Juan de Santo Matía in September 1567. Yet, fired as she was with the zeal for reform, her eyes sparkled with a youthful light. She was beautiful and spoke calmly but persuasively and to the point. Fray Juan, small and thin-faced, with sensitive features, was twenty-five.

Mother Teresa had been trying to win over Fray Pedro de Orozco. He had all the qualities she was looking for in the first Discalced Carmelite friar—young, personable and pious, and a high-achieving student at the University of Salamanca. She prayed ceaselessly to God to convince him that this was his calling, mortifying her flesh and asking her nuns to do the same.

Fray Pedro listened to her with the respect her growing fame merited. But he remained unconvinced. He considered it to be madness. Yet it made him think of his fellow student at Salamanca and brother in the Carmelite Order, Fray Juan de Santo Matía, who was then living with his family in Medina. It was in that town that they had both celebrated their first Mass on the feast of the Assumption of the Virgin. They were good friends. Indeed, Fray Pedro was the only person who knew of Juan's intention to leave the Carmelite Order and join the Carthusians of El Paular in Segovia. In fact, the superior of that monastery had already agreed to this. If Juan was prepared to do something as mad as that, Fray Pedro reasoned, he should be able to understand Mother Teresa's particular brand of madness.

Mother Teresa placed considerable importance on appearances. At first she was not impressed by Fray Juan de Santo Matía. Except for his sensitive expression, he appeared quite insignificant. Nevertheless, she began to tell him about the Reform and about their lives in the convent of San José in Ávila.

"I beg your pardon," Juan interrupted, "but I have already decided to join the Carthusians in Segovia."

"Why?" she inquired in surprise.

"Because in El Paular I believe I will find the kind of

life I seek. A cold, clear stream runs past its doors. Behind it rises the sierra, which remains snow-capped for much of the year, so that the air coming down from the mountains is very pure. For such tranquillity my soul yearns. There I think I will be able to pray."

"If it is as you say," La Madre replied calmly, "it would seem an earthly paradise. And if what you seek is sensual delight, then you may find it in El Paular. But if it is God you seek, do not expect to find Him there or anywhere but the place to which the guiding hand of His Holy Mother Our Lady of Mount Carmel has brought you. What I can offer you has little to do with such delights. It is but a tiny friary in a distant part of the country. Indeed, it is so remote that not even the people who live nearby know of its where-abouts. It took us a whole day to find it. We had to walk many miles hither and thither until we stumbled upon it at last. The house was in ruins, and in such a filthy state we could not stay the night. But whatever else it lacks, it has a good door, a double bedchamber in the garret, and a small kitchen. I have decided that this is to be the first friary for Discalced Carmelites, if there be any bold enough to answer to that name."

Juan was regarding her intently. He did not say a word.

"I will say this also", she continued. "My companion, Antonia del Espíritu Santo, who is far more virtuous than I, and no stranger to penance, could not reconcile herself to my decision to found the friary there. She could not believe that anyone, however good, would be able to abide living in such a place. And she advised me against it. Yet it is my unshakable conviction that this is where the first friary of Discalced Carmelites is to be. And the spiritual simplicity of those who dwell there will make up for what it lacks in beauty, for they will be unencumbered by all but God."

At this, Fray Juan sprang up and said:

"I will go. But let it be soon."

La Madre's heart leapt with joy because it meant that, like the Apostles, this diminutive friar was ready to leave everything behind at a stroke. And without further ado, she began to explain the rudiments of the Reform. It was important that there should be no misunderstanding about the self-mortification and the style of brotherhood involved. Fray Juan agreed to everything as if he already knew it, raising no objections.

They went on to talk about God, almost outdoing each other with the beauty of their words. They were so at ease it was as if they had known one another for years.

At the end of the interview, La Madre declared to her nuns that she had learned more from him than he from her.

"Even about the Reform, Mother?" asked one nun.

"Even about the Reform", she replied. "For the Reform is God's work. And this little friar is closer to God than I. Help me give thanks to Almighty God, Sisters, for now we have a friar and a half to begin the reform of the religious!"

The phrase "friar and a half" was thought to be an allusion to Fray Juan's diminutive stature. But the "half" was later clarified by one of Teresa's closest followers, María Evangelista, as referring to Father Antonio de Heredia. For as soon as Fray Juan had accepted, she decided to accept the prior of Medina. Nonetheless, she remained convinced that he had so few years left in him that he could be considered only half a friar.

Ana de San Bartolomé, one of the first nuns in the convent of San José in Ávila and another of Mother Teresa's closest followers, recounts:

> Shortly after this, in the parlor of the house in Medina, a length of coarse woolen cloth was cut for him. This was

to be made into his habit instead of the fine cloth used by mitigated Carmelites. When he took this habit, he changed his name to Fray Juan de la Cruz, for he loved the Cross of Christ above all things.

As La Madre wanted her friars to be learned, he returned to Salamanca to finish his studies. But he would come to Medina whenever he could to serve the nuns of the recently founded convent.

"One cloudless night," Ana de San Bartolomé continues,

when going to Valladolid in a covered cart, we were accompanied on the road by Fray Juan riding on a little donkey. As we journeyed under the stars, he talked about God and the virtuous life we were to lead as Discalced sisters. The beauty of his words so wrapped up our souls that, despite La Madre's inability to abide a weeping nun, we could not hold back our tears. The twenty-four-mile journey was to take us the whole night. Yet it went by in a trice. What we were most struck by, however, was that though he had only recently joined the Reform, he seemed to know as much about it as La Madre. A young peasant girl by the name of Francisca de Villalpando was journeying with us. She had often avowed that the last thing she wanted to be was a nun. That night she changed her mind and shortly afterward professed her vows in the Order.

When La Madre had gotten together the things needed for the foundation of the first Discalced friary, she asked Fray Juan whether it would be enough for the church and house.

"More than enough, Mother", he replied, without even glancing at the list.

According to the accounts of the house of Discalced Carmelites in Medina del Campo, the list consisted of some blankets, hourglasses for the regulation of monastic life, one or two pictures for the cells and a figure of Christ for the tiny church.

In all matters to do with the foundation process, Fray Juan deferred to Mother Teresa without question, believing God to have infused her with a zeal and the qualities necessary for this. In other areas, such as spirituality, self-mortification and penance, he did not hesitate to correct her. Sometimes he even went so far as to criticize her. And though she did not always take this very well, he never lost his patience. He would gently but firmly persevere, and in the end she would accept his reprimand.

Mother Teresa decided that Father Antonio de Heredia and Fray Juan de la Cruz would found the house together. It was to take Fray Antonio some time to extricate himself from his position as prior of the monastery in Medina, however. So La Madre, who was impatient to begin, instructed Fray Juan to go ahead and start work on the house on his own.

The house was in a place called Duruelo, a tiny hamlet in the province of Ávila with at most twenty inhabitants. It was so hidden away that it was all but impossible to find without asking for directions several times. Even then, not all the people of the area knew where it was. A gentleman from Ávila by the name of Don Rafael Mejía had made the abandoned farm worker's cottage over to Mother Teresa. Ignoring the warnings of her nuns that its remoteness and ruinous state would make it more trouble than it was worth, she had decided to accept the gift.

Fray Juan went by way of Río de Olmos, near the River Pisuerga, Valdestillas, Olmedo, Arévalo and Ávila. He walked at a fast pace, as though with a sense of urgency. He had nothing with him but the canvases, the figure of Christ and a small amount of money that had come from the dowry of a novice who had recently professed her vows. On the outskirts of Peñaranda he saw a man sitting by the side of the road. Beside the man lay something large and gray. As Fray Juan neared the man, he saw that he was weeping and that the gray thing he had seen was a donkey.

"Why do you weep, fellow?" Fray Juan inquired kindly as he came up.

"My donkey Sancho has just died", the man said through his tears. "He was the only thing I had left in all the world."

"Then you are fortunate indeed", Fray Juan said. "For if all that you had in the world is gone, all that remains is God."

"Do you make fun of me?" the man shouted.

"No indeed", Fray Juan replied. "I am in earnest. Will you tell me your story?"

The man began to tell the story of a hard life. He had been a soldier, had been taken prisoner by the Turks and had suffered much in captivity. But at last he had escaped. And thanks to the generosity of his captain, he had been able to buy the donkey. He had been on his way to his own village, where he intended to earn his living using the animal as a beast of burden.

"What work did you do as a prisoner?" Fray Juan asked.

"Stonemason", he replied. "We built the Pasha's palace."

Without hesitation Fray Juan said, "I can offer you something like that. Help me build a palace. But not for the Pasha, for God."

"What are you paying?" the man inquired, eyeing Fray Juan dubiously. In his rough serge habit he looked more like a beggar than a friar.

"First I will help you bury your donkey, for it has already begun to stink", said Fray Juan.

As they had no spade, they began to dig with an iron spike. It had been a hot, dry summer, and the earth was as hard as rock.

"My name is Fray Juan de la Cruz", he began as they worked. "I am on my way to a place called Duruelo. I don't know what I'll find when I get there. All I know is that I am going to Duruelo to build a palace to God and that Providence has put you on this road. For I confess I was beginning to wonder how I was going to build it on my own."

The man had stopped digging. He was leaning on his spike. It was a hot day, and he was breathing hard. He wiped his forehead with his sleeve, staring at Fray Juan, not quite sure he had heard right.

Fray Juan calmly continued, "I am a Carmelite. The friary I have been sent to Duruelo to found is to be dedicated to the Blessed Virgin Mary, who is our patron saint."

The man's expression cleared. He began to prod and scrape at the hard earth again.

"Spare your breath, Brother", the man said as he worked. "If Our Lady is involved in this, there is nothing more to be said. I am in her debt. And it seems the time has come to settle the score."

Fray Juan listened with great interest to the story of how he owed his life to the Blessed Virgin.

"Take care," Fray Juan warned, "for Our Lady has a habit of calling in such debts with interest. I will not deceive you. It will be hard work, and I cannot pay you. But I can offer you a place to lay your head at night and peace of mind in the knowledge that you will be doing God's work."

When some time later the man professed as a lay brother by the name of Fray Pedro de Cristo, Fray Juan reminded him of their meeting on the road to Duruelo. And he said that this was what he had meant about debts being called in with interest.

They reached Duruelo midway through October 1568.

As far as the eye could see, the land was one yellowing field of stubble. On the horizon the sky paled into a haze as it dissolved into the foothills of the Sierra de Gredos. The house was humble in the extreme. But Fray Juan was delighted to find a little stream running behind it. He loved the sound of running water. To him it was like the flow of life itself. On its banks stood a row of small trees. It turned out that these trees offered a nesting place for larks, whose twittering song the saint also loved.

Mother Teresa had given Fray Juan a set of plans that she had drawn up with her own hands, and a list of the jobs to be carried out. Fray Juan immediately began work with Pedro the stonemason. They turned the main part of the house into the church, the hayloft into the choir, and the only bedchamber into the dormitory.

They worked without stopping. Pedro's skill as a builder was considerable, and Fray Juan deferred to him in all building matters, meekly carrying out his instructions.

Francisco describes this episode in his account to Father Velasco as follows:

> It was inevitable that the fellow should have become a servant of Christ and the Blessed Virgin, Mother of Carmel. For it was impossible to spend time with my brother and remain unaffected. None who had dealings with him were unscathed by the fire in his soul.
>
> I visited Duruelo at about that time, for La Madre greatly desired to have news of her beloved son, knowing there were few more-remote places in the world. When I arrived, the work was already well in hand. For my part I did what I could. The place was certainly in the middle of nowhere. Until the arrival of the Discalced friars the people of those parts had been in dire need of God, having had no priest to serve them. I was also able to bring my brother and Fray

Pedro some food. God knows they needed it. Yet they got by with what little they had. There were days when they had still not broken fast by nightfall, for they did not put down their tools even to eat. Then the lay brother would go from one house to another in the neighborhood. And the good people would give him some bread, with which they made a thin soup seasoned with but a pinch of salt. Yet they would not have eaten it with greater satisfaction had it been roast pheasant.

For all its simplicity, the place had a charm of its own, tucked in a nook of a rolling valley studded with holm oaks. The friary, which they called "the palace", was as tidy a piece of work as I ever saw, for the lay brother had some skill in stonework. And bare though the church was, having no more adornment than the figure of Christ, it inspired devotion. How the laborers of those parts marveled to see the transformation they wrought on the old abandoned cottage. Whenever a number of them came together, Fray Juan would preach and then hear confessions. When the church was finished, the friars no longer had to go out and beg for food, for the country folk would bring it to them. But if they had more than they needed, Fray Juan would not accept their generosity, saying that they must live in poverty. Once we were invited by a laborer to dine at his master's house. This invitation Fray Juan politely declined. Later he told me he did not accept their charity because he needed no payment or thanks for doing God's work.

He only accepted bread, and then only if he could not avoid it, for the lay brother made a vegetable garden that provided them with all they needed. My brother used to say that Providence would answer all his needs. But what would have become of him if he hadn't met that lay brother, I do not know. Not only was the man a skilled builder, he also had some skill in the cultivation of plants, medicinal herbs and herbs for seasoning food. In all such matters Fray Juan

deferred to the lay brother's greater knowledge, doing his
bidding without question in the garden and in other matters
unrelated to the soul. Yet my brother always found a way
of wedding one to the other. And he would take every opportunity to reflect upon such things to their mutual benefit. Their first crop was garbanzos. As they were threshing
them, my brother said how sweet it was to work with these
mute little creatures. He saw the hand of God the Creator in
everything, even garbanzo beans, and he marveled greatly at
it. But still more greatly did I marvel at his words, by which
he endeavored to convey how much he loved the simplicity
of life in that remote corner, and how little he desired to
return to the hurly-burly of the world.

Though I never knew him to be discontented, I cannot
recall a time when he was happier than during this period.
I could not help thinking how proud our father would have
been of such a son. He already knew much about our father, but he never tired of hearing more. He also wanted
me to speak of him in the presence of the lay brother and
other friars, that they might learn how it is possible to live
a whole and perfect life in the bustle of the world. But, he
would add, he could not do so, for he was not cut out for
such a life. The only kind of life God had fitted him for
was an enclosed life. His humility was boundless, his most
fervent wish to discover the hidden treasures of the soul.
Yet he would take no credit for these, or be proud of them.
"There is no greater thief than the thief within", he would
say. And he would explain that God has placed certain qualities in our souls that cannot be taken away from us. But
through vanity and other attributes close to home, we revel
in them and claim them as our own, which is the same as
stealing from God. Thus we turn ourselves into thieves. He
would often exclaim, "God save us from ourselves!"

I spent a month or so in Duruelo and would have stayed
longer had not my obligations called me home. When I did

not go, Fray Juan was not slow to remind me of my duty. To reassure our mother, we sent her a letter by means of a muleteer from Mancera de Abajo, some three miles distance from Duruelo.

I also felt it my duty as his older brother to chide him for not writing to our mother more often. And with a stab of conscience he vowed to do so. He kept his word from then on and wrote such beautiful letters that they ravished us.

As long as I live, I will not forget those days that were all so alike but none the less memorable for that. Rising before dawn, we would go to the hamlet or tiny cluster of cottages. Then Fray Juan would begin to hear confessions until it was time for Mass, after which he would preach. At nightfall we would return to Duruelo. But if we met folk on our way, he would attend to each and every one. Thus it was often well after nightfall before we returned home. For my part, humble weaver that I am, I was very sensible of the honor he did me in allowing me to share in such things. Yet never was my sense of unworthiness at this honor so great as when he entreated me also to speak to the laborers. He bade me tell them how, for all our worldliness, we should love and serve God with all our heart and with all our mind. And he would say how pleased our Heavenly Father would be when He looked down and saw our work. And he commended me to it.

Chapter 10

From the Poverty of Duruelo
to the Turmoil of the
Convent of the Incarnation

The first Discalced Carmelite friary was formally established in Duruelo on the first Sunday of Advent, November 28, 1568. The father provincial at that time, Fray Alonso González, presided over the ceremony. This pious and deeply virtuous old man wept at the lowliness of the friary that restored the primitive rule, untempered by mitigation of any kind whatever. He was accompanied by three friars. The first was Fray Antonio de Heredia, who had at last succeeded in obtaining his release from the priorate of Medina del Campo. The second was a Conventual from Medina by the name of Father Lucas, who was coming for a trial period, as he did not know whether he would stand the test. Last came Fray José de Cristo, who had then received only minor orders.

They celebrated Mass. Then, in a simple ceremony before the father provincial, Fray Antonio de Heredia, Fray Juan de la Cruz and the deacon, Fray José, renounced the Carmelite rule mitigated by Eugene IV, vowing from then on to live in accordance with the primitive rule. The founding charter was then drawn up. Fray Juan himself signed this, using the name Juan de la Cruz (John of the Cross) for the first time. He wrote his name and drew the sign of the Cross, a signature he was to keep for the rest of his life. Fray Antonio de Heredia was appointed prior. Father Lucas also became a member of the community. He did not change his Franciscan habit, however, not because he did not want to but because he was ill, and Fray Juan told him it was not necessary. Fray Juan's uncertainty about this proved well founded. Not long after that the man's health obliged him to leave Duruelo. And shortly afterward he died. But he died with a deep sense of pride at having been one of the first friars in Duruelo, which he described as "a little corner of Heaven on earth".

The lay brother also decided to stay on in the community. But he thought long and hard about it. He could not understand why Fray Juan should be subordinate to someone who had done so little of the work on the friary.

"In that case, *you* should be prior," Fray Juan replied, "for you have laid more stones than the rest of us put together. If you think thus, then perhaps you should leave, for you have understood little of what we are about."

The man accepted this. Yet to begin with, when Fray Antonio de Heredia gave him an order, he would look to Fray Juan, as if waiting for a nod from him before carrying it out. One night at chapter the prior asked as usual if anything had been done that day that needed correction.

"Yes, Father", Fray Juan replied. "When Your Reverence tells Fray Pedro to do something, he looks at me, as if my eyes carried more weight than Your Reverence's commands. And if Your Reverence does not correct this, I shall go about with my eyes shut from now on so that I may not see Fray Pedro."

Fray Antonio had to contain his mirth as he corrected the fault. But in spite of his rustic directness, the lay brother was liked by all the friars. And he made an invaluable contribution to the community. Once, a neighboring farmer's mare became bloated. The animal would have died but for Fray Pedro, who knew exactly where to puncture the distension with a knitting needle. The farmer was so grateful that he gave the friars a donkey, which was extremely useful in the snow. Fray Pedro had the idea of fitting the beast with hay-filled saddlebags, into which the friars would thrust their bare feet as they trotted along the snow-covered paths. It was used principally by Fray Antonio de Heredia because of his age. The others would walk barefoot in all weathers. And but for a visit from Mother Teresa, they would have carried on doing so. She wrote to the father provincial, asking him to order them to wear rope-soled sandals. Her fear was that the devil might take advantage of what she regarded as excessive self-mortification to make them ill, which might endanger the whole project.

She visited Duruelo in March 1569. It had been a cold winter, and the roads and ways were still covered in snow. The first thing she saw when she finally got there, exhausted after the long journey, was the prior sweeping the church doorway.

"What is the meaning of this, Father Antonio?" she exclaimed joyfully. "What's become of your honor?"

"My honor?" he replied. "Why, I rue the day I ever had any."

Mother Teresa's secretary, Ana de San Bartolomé, was amazed at the poverty in which the prelates lived. Yet it was not wretchedness. The little friary was spotlessly clean and lovingly tended. There were flowers on the altars dedicated to the Blessed Virgin. As La Madre had not yet heard Mass that day, she asked Fray Juan to celebrate it. And, though she tried to hide it as usual, she experienced a rapture during the Mass in which she levitated. The nuns were accompanied by two merchants from Medina who were helping her with her houses. Fray Juan's sermon moved the merchants to tears. They had never heard Christ talked about in such language.

It was Father Antonio who told La Madre that Fray Juan was not going back to his straw mattress after matins but was remaining in prayer. And though in winter the snow would come in through a little window and fall on him where he knelt, he took no notice of it. La Madre reprimanded him for this. As she had authority over him only in matters concerning the foundation process, however, he ignored this too.

Ana de San Bartolomé comments:

> La Madre was delighted by her visit to Duruelo. Indeed, it gave her greater satisfaction than any of her convents. But she felt sorry for Fray Juan. His task accomplished, he had assumed that nothing remained but to live in the seclusion of Duruelo, letting the years pass in close union with God, cut off from the world.
>
> "Not just the world!" La Madre exclaimed. "Cut off from everything, including yourself! It is not up to you to say where you will live out the rest of your days. Nor have you earned that right. Your duty is to be in readiness to carry out whatever your superiors tell you to do."

The Reform of the Order had begun in earnest, and she could see he had a more important part to play in it than to minister to the good souls of Duruelo.

"And yet", Ana de San Bartolomé concludes,

> many benefits sprang from the folly of founding a house in that remote place. Some who were utterly without learning when Fray Juan came there ended up professing their vows in Carmel. One went to the Congo in Africa, and several others crossed the Ocean Sea. God be praised. But La Madre's prophetic words were soon borne out by events.

Nor could it have been otherwise, as it was God's work she was doing.

So it fell out that Fray Juan taught the first novices of the Discalced Reform, who came to Duruelo. In this they could have had no better teacher. And it was in this capacity that he went to Mancera, where a good house was founded thanks to the generosity of Don Luis de Toledo, the cousin of the Duke of Alba. There was already a fine church with a canvas brought back from the Low Countries. Here Fray Juan worked as spiritual director of sixteen novices. From thence he went to Pastrana. Thanks to the benevolence of the prince and princess of Eboli, La Madre founded two Discalced houses in Pastrana, the first a convent, the second a friary. Fray Juan also acted as spiritual director here. In this he was assisted by the lay brother from Duruelo. They journeyed barefoot to Pastrana, putting on their rope-soled sandals only as they entered the convent so as not to displease La Madre, for fear that she would report them to the father provincial. He then went to Alcalá as rector of the first Discalced college. From thence he went on to the convent of La Encarnación as its father confessor and vicar, where he was to remain for five years. It was during this period that we had most to do with him and benefited most from so sublime a soul. From all this we may see how short-lived was his dream of leading an enclosed life in Duruelo, to which he was never to return.

Fray Juan's vow of obedience to his superiors obliged him to modify his hopes and dreams. He was not alone in this. Mother Teresa too had founded the convent of San José intending to lead an enclosed life in Ávila. But her superiors would not allow it, and she had to go from place to place founding houses. She also had less important, but no less pressing, demands on her time. With her growing reputation as a saint, requests to visit people poured in. It was as if all they needed to be healed in body and soul was to touch her, like another Saint Roch. In 1582 a prelate of the Order asked her to visit the Duchess of Alba. The Duchess was about to give birth and wanted to be attended by someone who was already being spoken of as a saint, believing it would ensure a safe delivery. La Madre resented such requests. But in the end she agreed. The only time she openly disobeyed was when she was told to by Our Lord Himself.

The apostolic commissioner, Fray Pedro Fernández, whose authority came from Rome, decided that Mother Teresa should be appointed prioress of the convent of La Encarnación [the Incarnation] in Ávila. She was to restore order in it. Mother Teresa had always loved this convent. After all, she had spent twenty-five years of her life there and received many favors from God, including the call to undertake the Reform of the Order. She had left it to found the convent of San José in the brown habit and white cowl of the Discalced Order. The convent of the Incarnation, Ávila's most famous religious house, was in the north of the city, some five hundred yards from the city wall, opposite the Carmen Gate. Young women flocked to it to profess their vows, some with true vocations, others because they did not know what else to do. The ecclesiastical dignitary who had authorized its construction described it as "a most proper and fitting place for nuns to dwell, a quiet place with gardens and an abundance of water for the recreation and well-being of its inhabitants".

But standards of monastic life in the Incarnation had taken a serious turn for the worse. The cause of this is unclear. It might have been a lack of vocation on the part of the nuns. Or it might have been due to the famine that gripped Castile at that time. The fact remains that the only rule in the convent was the whim of the most unruly. Consequently, those who wanted to live the rule righteously could not do so. The convent's larders were bare. The nuns did not eat in the refectory. Each ate what she could in her own cell. Those from wealthier families had food delivered to them by their relatives. The poorer nuns, meanwhile, went hungry. Saint Paul might almost have been writing about La Encarnación in the first of his letters to the Corinthians [11:21]: "For every one taketh before his own supper to eat. And one indeed is hungry, and another is drunk."

With the constant comings and goings of relatives and even of the nuns themselves, monastic practices had become dangerously lax. Liaisons far removed from the love of those who called themselves brides of Christ were being conducted within the walls of the convent. When in 1571 Mother Teresa received the apostolic commissioner's request to take the job of prioress of the Incarnation, she already knew this. Disturbed by what was going on there, she was reluctant to take up the post. If she were to accept, she would have no time for her own houses, some of which had only just been founded. Besides, her knowledge of human nature and monastic life told her that the more-uncompromising nuns were not likely to accept a prioress appointed by the apostolic commissioner—and still less, one who might make them adopt the rigorous rule of the Discalced nuns.

She had decided to write to Fray Pedro Fernández explaining her reasons for turning down the offer when one day, while deep in prayer, Our Lord spoke to her.

"These are my sisters in the Incarnation convent", He said. "Why do you hesitate?"

With deep humility she replied that she was worried she would have no time for the other houses He had encouraged her to found.

"Don't be so fainthearted", He continued. "Listen to

what I want. It's not as hard as you think. As for your concerns to do with the other houses, it will all turn out well in the end. Do not resist me. My power is very great."

Mother Teresa was on speaking terms with Our Lord at the time, often conversing with Him in prayer. Her doubts dispelled, she told the apostolic commissioner she was at his disposal.

On October 6, 1571, she presented herself at the gates of the convent. She was accompanied by the father provincial, Fray Angel de Salazar. He had brought the chief magistrate with him and a troop of bailiffs to force entry if necessary. The nuns greeted her with insults punishable by excommunication. The father provincial saw this but did not dare give the order to break down the gate. Instead, he ordered a bailiff to force the lower choir door with a crowbar. But some of the more daring nuns raised the alarm. They barred the way with their own bodies and redoubled their insults.

Mother Teresa sat on a bench by the church door, calmly reciting the rosary. She seemed quite unperturbed by what was going on. The provincial, on the other hand, was alarmed by the uproar. A small crowd had begun to gather at the convent gate.

"For all our sakes," he began, "I think we'd better tell the apostolic commissioner that it will not be possible to proceed with your appointment."

"You might convince the apostolic commissioner," Mother Teresa calmly replied, "but not Our Lord Jesus Christ."

The father provincial was a good man. But he had no idea what Mother Teresa was talking about. Turning back to the main gate, which was still barricaded by the nuns, he said, "As it is clear that you do not want Mother Teresa de Jesús . . ."

His words were cut short by a loud cry from a nun who

had taken a vow of silence. As she had never broken this, she was believed by many to be mute.

"We do want her!" the nun cried out. "We love La Madre!"

Ana de San Bartolomé later comments, "So arresting was this most unexpected of outbursts that it was followed by a silence like that which the passing of an angel might produce."

Catalina de Castro, the nun presumed mute, took advantage of this silence to begin a solemn *Te Deum*. One by one the other nuns joined in, until only a handful of the protestors remained. The community numbered 130 nuns. In the end over a hundred gladly accepted their new prioress.

Mother Teresa knew she had to tackle the convent's spiritual poverty. First, however, she would do something about its material poverty.

"How much more patiently does God await souls than do people the filling of their bellies", she pronounced. "With the exception of those who fast for virtuous reasons, what hope is there for the souls of the hungry?"

In spite of her worsening health, she began to go out, asking anyone she could think of for alms. She called on Doña María de Mendoza, Doña Magdalena de Ulloa and even the Duchess of Alba. These devout noblewomen did what they could. For her own part, Mother Teresa would not touch a piece of bread until there was enough for all the nuns. This went on for three months. It was to be a further three before they were able to supplement their diet of bread and water with a thin goat's milk gruel.

Ana de San Bartolomé comments:

> It troubled us deeply that La Madre would not allow a morsel of the convent's bread to pass her lips. She did this so that

the nuns might not go without. If she did eat, she would say it gave her stomach pains. But what was our wonder when, on a visit to the house of Doña María de Mendoza, or one of the other great ladies who helped us, she declined to eat any of the food they had provided, saying that if her nuns had nothing to eat, she too would go without. If she did accept a little, it was to avoid giving offense, and then she barely touched it, saying she had just eaten. The result of these visits, and the privation we endured, was that she raised enough money to enable us to eat in the refectory again. And that was the beginning of the restoration of order to the life of the convent. But it is my belief that this period did much harm to La Madre's health, which was only precarious at best.

By the time Mother Teresa had put the convent's financial affairs in order, she had become ill. She suffered from fevers that confined her to bed and made it impossible to attend Mass unless supported by two nuns. At the same time her gift of prayer dried up. With her lines of communication cut off, she had no idea how to solve the problem of the nuns. Their material needs might have been dealt with, but their spiritual situation was as chaotic as ever.

"This place," she commented wryly, "Ávila, I mean, has taken so much out of me that I can scarcely think of it as my birthplace."

One day a possible reason for God's silence occurred to her. Maybe He was trying to tell her He wanted her to concentrate on the community's material needs and leave spiritual matters to more sophisticated souls than hers. This thought prompted her to write to Fray Juan de la Cruz, who was rector of the Carmelite school in Alcalá de Henares at the time.

"But the devil", Ana de San Bartolomé continues,

> did not want the saint to come where he was so sorely
> needed. At any rate, the apostolic commissioner, who had
> hitherto given his assent in all matters concerning La Madre,
> refused on this occasion. His reason was that it was unheard
> of for a Discalced friar to be appointed chaplain of a con-
> vent whose spiritual directors had always been unreformed
> friars. La Madre pleaded with him however, and in the end
> he agreed.

When Fray Juan heard of the apostolic commissioner's decision and the lengths Mother Teresa had gone to because
of her high regard for him, he commented, "It is a strange
regard that would send me into a wasp's nest."

Knowing he had little choice, however, he accepted and
presented himself at the convent of the Incarnation in late
spring of 1572.

Mother Teresa was overjoyed, singing his praises incessantly and telling her nuns that she had brought a saint to be
their father confessor. Unfortunately, this only intimidated
many of the nuns, who confused sanctity with severity. The
result was that at first they refused to go to his confessional.

Fray Juan had just turned thirty. He was small. His face,
though thin and weather-beaten, was kindly. His grave features were often lit up by a warm smile. But above all, he
was patient. Every afternoon, he would sit quietly in his
confessional in the church. He did not mind how long it
took for his first penitent to come to him. The nuns fluttered
around his confessional but would invariably end up going
to one of the confessionals attended by the unreformed fathers, sometimes called "fathers of the cloth". We shall re-
fer to these from now on as the "Calced", as distinct from

the discalced fathers of the Reform, who wore rough serge habits.

This angered Mother Teresa. But nothing would have made her compel them in their choice of confessor.

One day she said with a heavy sigh:

"I'm sorry to have brought you here, Father. You'd better start thinking about returning to Alcalá."

"Signa apostolatus nostri facta sunt super vos in omni patientia, in signis et prodigiis et virtutibus", he replied. He would often use Latin when reproaching her. "Do you understand, Mother?" he added.

"I understand only that you know far more Latin than this nun. I can just about string two or three words together in my native Castilian. But when my little Seneca talks to me in Latin, I tremble, for then I know I must have done something wrong. Be so good as to tell me what it means."

Fray Juan replied, "It is the Apostle to the Gentiles in his letter to the Corinthians, in which he says that patience is mightier than miracles. For if things don't go as you want, you quickly lose patience. Have you forgotten that patience is a clearer sign of the Apostle than the raising of the dead? With patience even the cedars of Lebanon can be toppled. I for one do not hold these nuns to be so dead that they cannot be brought back to life. Nor do I think them harder to topple than the cedars of Lebanon."

These words of her "little Seneca" made a deep impression on Mother Teresa, particularly when the next day a nun entered Fray Juan's confessional. She was followed by every nun in the convent.

Angela de Cuñiga was a young, timid, recently professed nun. Her mind was apt to wander in the choir, and she frequently had to be reprimanded for not following prayers, especially when sung. Being obedient and sweet natured, however, she had been allowed to profess her vows. That afternoon she came into the church in a daydream as usual, to make her confession.

As she stood next to the confessional in which Fray Juan patiently sat, she asked one of her companions, "Is this the Discalced father, the barefoot one?"

Fray Juan immediately replied, "I am shod, Sister."

This was no lie. He was in fact wearing the rope-soled sandals he wore when walking on rough ground.

Trembling, the young nun fell to her knees when she realized to whom the voice belonged. But Fray Juan spoke to her gently, and Angela de Cuñiga at last confessed to him that all the nuns were afraid of him because he was said to be a saint.

"I am no saint, Sister", Fray Juan assured her. "But the more virtuous the confessor, the more lenient he will be. And the less likely to be shocked, for the better he will understand our human frailty."

Angela de Cuñiga emerged from the confessional deeply comforted. She became very attached to Fray Juan and was one of his most devoted penitents. She later professed in the Discalced Order. In time she conquered her tendency to be distracted and ended up as head chantress of the convent of Beas.

Fray Juan, and the lay brother who had accompanied him, took up residence in the convent of Our Lady of Carmel by the north wall of the city. Here he lived in perfect harmony with the Calced fathers. The bitter fratricidal struggle that was to tear the two sides apart had not yet begun. Encouraged by Angela de Cuñiga's experience, the other nuns began to visit his confessional in preference to those of the Calced fathers. When Mother Teresa realized what was happening, she moved him to a tiny bothy, a hut, in the garden of the convent, so that he could be nearer his penitents. From there he would be able to attend them at any time of day or night. Indeed, there were some very elderly nuns, and on several occasions he had to administer the last rites in the middle of the night. But her decision may also have been influenced by the jealousy that the new chaplain's growing fame had awakened in the Calced fathers.

Apart from a stone bench and a blanket, on which Fray Juan slept, the bothy was completely bare. Fray Juan was delighted with it. Indeed, he liked it so much that when he heard Mother Teresa had asked Doña María de Mendoza for a bed for the bothy, he told her he did not want it. Living in the bare cell with nothing but his few possessions, he could imagine he was in a Discalced friary again.

"I don't suppose you dream much on that bench, Father", La Madre said drily.

Fray Juan replied, "Don't shepherds lie on the hard rock to tend their flocks? Why not I?"

He tended his flock lovingly but no less exigently for that. He was always extremely attentive to their needs and was distressed by the conditions with which some of them had to endure. One day as he was going into the convent he saw a nun sweeping the floor of the cloister in her bare feet.

"Sister," he began, "should you be dressed like that and doing such penance in this holy place?"

The young nun breathlessly replied that she was not barefoot by choice or for virtuous reasons but because she could not afford to buy any shoes.

Although it was the confessional hour and there were many penitents waiting, Fray Juan turned on his heel and went out to beg for alms. He did not return until he had bought a good pair of shoes for the young nun.

When his penitents needed correction, however, he did

not hold back. He reminded them again and again of the words of Pope Pius II, who said that a wayward friar or nun was more dangerous than the devil himself.

The convent's most serious problem was the bustle of its parlors and visiting chambers, so at variance with the contemplative retreat demanded by the Carmelite vocation. Although Mother Teresa had forbidden going out or receiving visitors, there were so many nuns that some persisted in these habits. Among these was Doña Ana de Mendiola y Cuevar, a nun of noble birth with a large cell. It had its own kitchen and a smaller cell for a novice who was effectively her servant.

Haughty, imperious, strikingly beautiful and notoriously wealthy, it was a mystery why Doña Ana had professed her vows in the Carmelite Order. She certainly showed no inclination to fulfill her vows. It seems she was being visited by a wealthy gentleman who claimed to be her relative, though how they were related was also a mystery. It was obvious to everyone that he was in love with the beautiful nun. He felt the amount of money he was giving the convent gave him the right to visit her. Though his attentions were common knowledge and a great scandal, Doña Ana permitted them because of the dire situation of the convent's finances.

Fray Juan was not responsible for the convent's affairs, but only for the souls of its sisters. One day, after many hours of prayer and penance, he succeeded in persuading Doña Ana to kneel in his confessional and lay bare her soul to him. Because of the confidentiality of the confessional, what was said on this occasion is not known. But shortly after this, La Madre advised him not to waste any more time on her. As Doña Ana had not yet professed her final vows, Mother Teresa had told her she was free to leave the convent and marry whom she chose.

"What?" Fray Juan said in alarm. "Take one of Christ's brides from Him and give her to the devil himself?"

Though Fray Juan did not pull any punches, Mother Teresa believed him to possess a wisdom beyond that of mere mortals. He had a special sense about the genuineness of vocations. A prioress had only to express a vague doubt about a novice's vocation to be certain of a letter from him. He even gained a reputation as a matchmaker. He would speak to the friends and relatives of novices or would-be nuns to see if he could find a good match for them. But if he believed there to be a true vocation, he would wrestle with the devil himself to ensure it was not lost. And, as we shall see, he ended up exorcising many souls consecrated to God.

Doña Ana de Mendiola may not have been in league with the devil, but she came perilously close to it. It emerged that the gentleman in question was engaged to a Portuguese lady, a fact he had omitted to mention, and he was interested in Doña Ana for only one thing. He wanted to boast about his sacrilegious conquest. He later became a Lutheran in Valladolid and escaped burning at the stake only by fleeing to Flanders to join others of his own kind. Few if any of the nuns of the Incarnation convent were surprised by this news. It was said a faint smell of sulfur followed him wherever he went.

"Money is always tinged with the smell of sulfur", Fray Juan observed wryly. "Indeed, it is not long since the convent's own coffers were tainted with that smell, courtship having been condoned in return for money."

After her third visit to Fray Juan's confessional, Doña Ana promised she would never again receive her suitor. Weeping piteously, she vowed to be a good nun and not deviate from the rule in the smallest degree, even if it meant she must give up her servants and visits from her relatives.

It did not take the gentleman long to find out who was responsible for his being barred from the convent. In the heat of his lascivious passion, he swore to take revenge on the chaplain.

One dark night the gentleman in question and his servant waited for Fray Juan in the vegetable garden near the bothy. While the servant pinioned Fray Juan's arms, the gentleman beat him with the flat of his sword.

"This is the devil's work", said Fray Juan to the servant, without flinching as the blows rained down on him. "Take no part in it. And to spare your conscience, go in peace. I will not move from this place, do your master what he will."

The servant took to his heels in astonishment. The gentleman, meanwhile, continued to beat Fray Juan. He would have gone on until he had killed Fray Juan or left him for dead had it not been for the lay brother who heard the din and came to see what all the commotion was about. Fray Juan forbade him to breathe a word about the incident. When the next day Mother Teresa asked him how he had gotten the livid weals on his face, he replied:

"I was set upon by ruffians. They must have mistaken me for a rich man and tried to rob me."

"Not even a blind man would mistake you for a rich man, Father", she replied. And she ordered him as prioress to tell her the truth in case it affected the running of the convent. The saint duly confessed.

Mother Teresa comments:

He assured me the blows had been sweet, like Saint Stephen's stones, for they were the price of delivering a soul from evil. He was referring to Doña Ana de Mendiola, his devoted penitent. Indeed, she became so devout that she joined us in the Reform. And in time, once she had overcome her haughtiness, she rose to the position of mistress of novices in Córdoba.

Chapter 11

The Devil and Fray Juan de la Cruz

During the two years for which Mother Teresa was prioress of the Incarnation convent, she saw to it that her confessors, whether Calced or Discalced, had no contact whatsoever with the nuns. The only exceptions were in the confessional and the parlor, as long as it was divided by a sturdy grille. In this she was always the first to set an example.

Fray Juan shared her views about this. He spoke to his friars on the subject, reminding them of the words of Francisco de Osuna, whom Mother Teresa had urged him to study in depth. According to Osuna, "The devil sends his battalions against God's servants. His greatest champion is lust. Lust is armed with all the weapons required for victory and assails persons of all type and rank, of all ages, the beautiful and the ugly, the great and the small, the wise and the sick—in short, all mankind."

In the cause for the beatification of Fray Juan de la Cruz, Beatriz de Ocampo, a nun of the Incarnation convent, stated: "We all trusted him completely. Even when in the presence of a beautiful nun, there was no change in him whatsoever. It was as if he were not a man."

His brother Francisco must have read this comment, for he alludes to it in his own account:

> It is my belief that when Doña Beatriz de Ocampo said of my brother that it was as if he were not a man, she was comparing him to the angels. If so, she was mistaken, in this

respect at least, for he was no angel. He was a saint. And
saints are made of flesh and blood. Nor was the Revered
Fray Juan altogether exempt from the assaults of the devil
in the matter of lust. Indeed, none has ever been so but
Our Lord Jesus Christ, who was human in every respect
save one, that of sin. But here none escapes the torment of
such longings. Even Saint Paul speaks of "the thorn in the
flesh", by which he was surely referring to this evil. The
Revered Fray Juan was deeply troubled by the scourge of
the *alumbrados*. He described this grave offense against God
as concealed spiritual lust that subsequently turns into carnal
lust. I say it troubled him because he was himself subjected
to it and strove against it. Even as a student in Salamanca,
he characterized these heretics as a perversion of the true
mysticism of Saint Dionysus, Saint Gregory and other great
Fathers of the Church.

The *alumbrados* believed that close union with God could
be achieved by annihilating the faculties of the soul. For this
enables us to get rid of the burden of free will, and thus responsibility for our actions. This conveniently removes any
concern about temptation of any kind, however base. For
the soul that is bound to God cannot sin. Nor can it desire
or love anything but what God Himself has created or desires. And if it is God's wish that men and women should
come together and become one flesh, what harm is there
in that union being between men and women consecrated
to God? Would not their offspring be very holy? Not all
the *alumbrados* thought like this. But there were some who
started out hoping to arrive at union with God by a mystical
route and ended up thinking that sublime carnal union was
acceptable to God.

On the subject of lust and temptation, Fray Juan had a
great tussle with the devil. This began with a nun from the

Augustinian convent of Our Lady of Grace in Ávila, where Mother Teresa had been a pupil at the age of sixteen.

Her name was María de Olivares. She had been a pupil in that convent since the age of five. Despite being practically illiterate and having no great love of books, the day after she professed her novice's vows, she began to recite passages from the Scriptures. She also gave commentaries on them in an enraptured state. This frightened some and awed others. The superiors of the convent did not know what to do. They agreed that this knowledge must be inspired, but whether divinely or demonically, they could not say. "There is no shortage of doctors in our Holy Mother Church", said the prioress sagely.

It was a wealthy convent with many nuns of noble birth. So she was able to send for the best in Christendom. The theologians of Salamanca, Mancio de Corpus Christi, Bartolomé de Medina, Juan de Guevara and Fray Luis de León, duly marched into the parlor of Our Lady of Grace. Fray Luis had just been released from prison, his intellectual reputation hugely enhanced by his recent triumph over the Inquisition. His arrival in Ávila was received with ecstatic enthusiasm. All without exception were convinced of the nun's holiness. All agreed that her utterances did not run counter to the teaching of Holy Mother Church. Fray Luis de León, the most authoritative of all, stated that it seemed to have a good spiritual feel. "But, if not," he added, "time will tell."

But the prioress felt she could not afford to wait. The whole of Ávila was in an uproar about the phenomenon. There were people sleeping outside the gates of the convent. Believing the nun in question to be a saint, they were hoping to catch a glimpse of her and ask her special favors. In the end the prioress wrote to Mother Teresa to see if Fray Juan de la Cruz would be willing to speak to the nun.

"What can I add to what has already been said by those who were my own teachers?" he observed.

Later he wrote to his friend in Segovia, Father Diego de Jesús:

> I confess I was afraid to become involved in the business with María de Olivares. For if God was not speaking through her, it must be the devil. And as you well know, the devil can be cast out only by means of exorcism, after which he always takes his revenge. For this reason I shall henceforward teach that friars who shy away from taking on the devil for fear of his reprisals gravely offend against God. For thus do they enable him to steal souls from God.

He declined the request to go and see the nun. But at Mother Teresa's insistence, he agreed to go. La Madre was used to dealing with the devil. Her terrifying vision of hell had spurred her on to greater religiosity. In this way she hoped to save many souls from damnation. She was suspicious of the kind of raptures María de Olivares was said to be experiencing. And she could see no reason why Our Lord should be making her recite Holy Writ.

Fray Juan asked Fray Pedro de Cristo, the lay brother who had helped him with the Duruelo foundation, to go with him on his first visit to the convent of Our Lady of Grace. With the exception of the confessional, it was Fray Juan's strict rule never to be with any woman, nun or otherwise, unless accompanied by another friar.

The way from the Incarnation to the convent of Our Lady of Grace was long and uneven. They had to skirt the city walls, following a narrow, and in parts treacherous, path. It wound its way behind the cathedral and up to the gate of the alcazar, ending in a steep descent.

Fray Pedro was later to describe this:

> I had to take Fray Juan by the arm several times to avoid a headlong fall. He walked as if in a trance. He was deep in prayer and pale as a ghost. When I spoke to him to tell him to mind his step, he paid me no heed. He did not even look at me. In his right hand he held an iron crucifix, which he clutched so hard it made his hand bleed.

The superiors, including the father general of the Order himself, were waiting for them at the convent. The father general, who knew nothing about Fray Juan, was surprised that the nuns should have so much faith in a friar of such unprepossessing appearance. He looked for all the world as if he were at death's door.

Fray Juan and the lay brother were shown into a parlor, where María de Olivares waited. She was a lovely young woman of twenty with an air of blithe humility and an ethereal, almost angelic, quality.

In the same calm, measured tone he used in the confessional, Fray Juan began to talk to her. He questioned her about the Bible. She answered each question correctly. Now and then he commented on her answers, and she responded with comments of her own. They had been engaged in this kind of game for an hour or so when Fray Juan said:

"Now, my child, let us consider the cornerstone of our faith. Be so good as to translate this passage from Saint John's Gospel: *Verbum caro factum est et habitavit in nobis.*"

"And the Word was made flesh and dwelt among you", the nun translated without hesitation.

"How so *you*?," pounced Fray Juan. "The Apostle says among *us*."

"He was made flesh and dwelt among *you*, not us . . ."

shrieked the demons that possessed the unfortunate young woman.

The lay brother was later to recount:

At this, a shiver ran through me from head to toe.

Fray Pedro instinctively made the sign of the Cross. He had to fight to prevent himself from running out of the room. Fray Juan, on the other hand, was calmer than ever. He tried to soothe the young woman. He told her that it was within her power to turn the *you* into *us* and that he could help her to do this.

When he emerged, he said to the father general and the other prelates, "Your Reverences, the nun is bedeviled."

After a moment, the father general asked sternly, "Are you certain?"

Fray Juan was.

"You had better be, Father", said the father general. "For if you are right, we shall have no choice but to denounce her to the Inquisition."

Fray Juan calmly replied: "Some, I grant you, are possessed because they stubbornly refuse to forsake sin. But there are others whom God has allowed to become innocent victims in order to teach us patience, humility and self-mortification. Considering the age at which María de Olivares entered the convent, I would say she falls into the latter category. Before we deliver her into the hands of the Holy Office, should we not at least try to help her?"

The father general agreed and gave his permission for an exorcism. The nuns were not convinced of the need. The next day Fray Juan ordered María de Olivares' nightgown to be fetched. In the presence of the prioress and the other nuns, he solemnly blessed the garment as he recited the rite of exorcism. That night, when the unfortunate girl put on her nightgown, she began to scream. And to the terror of the watching nuns, she tore it off and flung it as far away from her as she could, saying that it burned her.

This settled any remaining doubts. Those who had been most sceptical immediately began to demand she be turned over to the Inquisition. Satan could not be allowed to live cheek by jowl with them in the convent.

"Is this your compassion, not to say ignorance?" Fray Juan thundered. "Have you forgotten the devil is always in our midst, stalking us like a roaring lion? Do you not know", he went on more calmly, "that Satan is behind all temptation, no matter how innocent it may seem? God permits Satan to do extraordinary things, not so we will burn the victim at the stake, which has no effect whatsoever on the devil and his minions, but to test our compassion."

The Augustinian sisters would not be pacified, however. They continued to clamor that María de Olivares must be removed and handed over to the Inquisition. In the end Mother Teresa herself had to intervene.

"Demons grow bold when they see we are afraid", she reasoned. "However, if we scorn them, they become cowardly and seemingly powerless. They tempt me ceaselessly. Yet, if I put my trust in the power of Our Savior Jesus Christ and pay them no more heed than a few flies, though they buzz around me, and may even vex me, they are harmless enough."

This seemed to satisfy the nuns. But when Fray Juan came to the convent to perform the exorcisms, they kept away. The bellows the devil emitted through the mouth of his victim would have struck terror into the heart of all but the bravest. At one point he picked her up and turned her upside down, her head lolling from side to side. This time the lay brother did run from the room, leaving Fray Juan alone.

After this, Fray Juan asked Francisco de los Ángeles, a lay porter from the Carmelite convent, to accompany him on these exorcisms. He may not have been the brightest of brothers, but he was devout and fearless. Sometimes, for special exorcisms, Fray Juan requested the assistance of two Carmelite friars, Fray Gabriel Bautista and Fray Pedro de la Purificación.

The exorcisms continued for three months. María's demons were not only tenacious but cunning. Sometimes they would pretend to have given up and left her. Then María de Olivares would appear docile. She would be unable to recite anything but the common prayers and remember nothing of what she had experienced. On their return, however, finding the house swept clean, her demons would reenter with redoubled fury, to the terror of those who had thought her cured—all except Fray Juan. Quite unperturbed, he calmly resumed his exorcisms. He limited himself to those recommended by the book of the rites of exorcism, mainly prayers, though he did not reject the sprinkling of holy water or Gregorian chant, which María's demons could not abide.

The day finally came when Fray Juan thought they had won. After a prolonged spate of howling and bellowing, María gave a gentle sob and began to speak in her normal voice.

"I was six when I gave my soul to him", she began. "We made a kind of pact. I pricked my arm until it bled. And using my own blood as ink, I declared myself his."

At this she began to weep.

"Tell me everything, my child", Fray Juan said quietly. "Brother Francisco," he continued, turning to the lay brother, "you may leave us. We will continue in the church, where I will hear Sister María's confession."

On their way to the confessional María de Olivares stopped. Looking straight into Fray Juan's eyes, she began to talk to him softly. She told him how much good he was doing her soul and other things he found so flattering that they made his head spin. Before him stood a young, beautiful woman, with all the seductiveness needed to overthrow the saintliest of men. With a show of undying gratitude, she fell to her knees and began to kiss his hands and other parts of his body. Fray Juan suddenly realized what was going on. He tried to free himself from her grasp, but she seemed to have the strength of ten men.

There ensued a terrible struggle between the spirit and the flesh. For a moment it seemed as if the flesh would win. Fearing the temptation would prove too much for him, Fray Juan called on Our Lady of Mount Carmel for strength. He managed to free one of his hands and thrust it into the flame of a candle, holding it there until his skin crackled and he smelled burning flesh. Then with his burned hand he fumbled for a bottle of holy water, which he always had with him in his exorcisms. He managed to sprinkle some over the possessed novice. She immediately began to foam at the mouth. Only then as she lay on the floor in convulsions was he able to shout for help. His calls were quickly answered by the lay brother and several nuns. Yet between them all, they were unable to overpower her.

"Did the devil do that to you, Father?" Mother Teresa inquired in alarm when she saw his terrible burns.

He replied: "No, Mother, the flesh. What the devil could not do, the flesh came within a hair's breadth of doing. But if we ask our Mother in Heaven for help, neither can prevail."

The devil persevered with María de Olivares for a while. Fray Juan was grateful for what he had learned. It was to serve him well in future exorcisms. At a time of universal religious belief, the devil had to work harder to get the better of God's servants. Fray Juan became famous as an exorcist. On one occasion not long before his death, when exorcising an eminent nobleman, the devil said in the man's voice: "With the exception of Saint Basil, none has fought me harder than Brother John of the Cross, Discalced Carmelite."

One of the things Fray Juan learned from this episode was that revenge, no Christian virtue, was a dish of which the devil was very fond—a dish he did his utmost to serve to anyone who managed to tear a captive from his clutches. Another was that you could tell when the devil had abandoned a victim because he would turn his attentions on someone else.

In the case of María de Olivares, these were the last words the devil uttered through the unfortunate girl's mouth: "Puny friar, since this fool no longer values the pleasure of my company, I will await you elsewhere."

Knowing this to be the devil's parting shot, Fray Juan told the prioress that the novice was cured. He was not mistaken. María de Olivares became an excellent nun. She had no special gifts and barely any knowledge of the Bible. But she was blessed with a love of the old, the sick, and little children, particularly those who had been abandoned. She was given the care of the old nuns in the convent and would spend whole nights at the bedsides of those who were near death.

But the story of the possessed young nun was well known in Ávila. To avoid unwelcome curiosity, she moved to another convent in Salamanca. There she died at the age of forty in the odor of sanctity.

No sooner had the demons left María de Olivares than they turned their attentions on the little bothy in the garden of the Incarnation. They set about making Fray Juan's life as difficult as possible.

"They cannot touch my soul," he said to La Madre, "for that belongs to God. And against Him they are powerless. But to my body, which is mine and mine alone, they can do some harm."

They came at night, keeping him awake. The next day he would find it hard to get up. In the small hours of the bitterly cold Ávila nights, they would pull off his blanket, leaving him uncovered and shivering uncontrollably. He was amazed he had not died of pneumonia. He asked the lay brother to tie his blanket down firmly. And although he felt them tugging at it, they could not pull it off. Then, giving thanks to the Blessed Virgin, despite the jostling to which he was subjected, he finally managed to sleep.

One night he heard shouting at the door. This was not unusual. He was often called on to attend the dying in the night. He opened the door, but no one was there. The shouts also woke the lay brother, who thought the voices human, not demonic. They wondered whether it might have been one of the saint's many enemies. A growing number of people were opposed to the order he was establishing in the convent. These included some gentleman with dishonorable intentions toward the nuns.

The following night the same thing happened. They decided that the porter, a burly man by the name of Fray Francisco de los Ángeles and Father Pedro de la Purificación, who was well known to be a sensible person, should come and sleep in the bothy. They set a watch. This time there were blows on the door. These were accompanied by the sounds of running up and down outside and the clatter of some-

The Fire of Love

thing like picks and shovels. When they opened the door, no one was there.

The noises were so lifelike that Fray Pedro de la Purificación was convinced they had been made by people.

"Probably thieves", he said. (The garden had once been a Moorish cemetery. The Moors were said to have been buried with their swords, which were often encrusted with precious stones.)

Fray Juan agreed this was more than likely. They posted an armed watchman in the garden. As it happened, there was a heavy snowfall that night and the garden was under several inches of snow. It was a cold, clear night, the fresh snow fine and powdery. As before, they were woken by the noise of banging on the door. The watchman threw open the window and shouted:

"Who's there? Show yourselves in the name of the king or I'll fire!"

No reply came. He fired once into the air and a second time in the direction of the noises. There was a cry as if someone had been hit, and the sound of people running away.

When they went out, however, though it was a clear, moonlit night, there were no footprints to be seen on the pristine snow. Fray Juan was the only one who was not surprised.

"Now that we know what we are dealing with," he said, "we can go back to bed. There's nothing to fear. We must simply get used to sleeping through the din our little devils make."

He called them his "little devils" to belittle them in the eyes of anyone who might be afraid of them.

"Yet", he added, "it would be as well to respect them,

above all when they assail our carnal passion. If pursued as God intends, this can lead to great glory. But if it is disordered, the glory is all Satan's."

In his account to Father Velasco, Fray Juan's brother Francisco alludes to this episode as follows:

> The love the Revered Fray Juan felt for our mother was sublime in the extreme. He would say that after the Holy Trinity and the Blessed Virgin, there was no one he loved more. As soon as he heard that she was ill with a fever, or some other illness, he would come to Medina. Not once, but many times, whatever the weather, or the state of the roads. He almost always walked. Very occasionally he journeyed on a little donkey. But he was an exceedingly good walker, and indeed he went at such a pace that far younger and stronger men were hard put to it to keep up with him. I accompanied him on one occasion when he was returning from Medina to Ávila. I did this not merely to help him on the road but because of the delight I felt in his company.

Here, the amanuensis, Francisco de la Peña, a Franciscan of the Third Order of Penitence, interjects:

> Francisco de Yepes would not permit us to set down in his account what is common knowledge among those who knew the Yepes family, namely, that the Revered Fray Juan de la Cruz considered his brother to be a greater saint than he. He would often say he had learned more from him than from countless theological treatises. And it is our opinion that when the time comes to revise this account, when both have gone to their eternal rest, this should be made known.

Francisco's account continues:

> As we neared Ávila, he told me he could not give me lodging in his little cottage in the garden. When I asked him why,

he replied that it was because of some troublesome little demons who were trying to stop its inhabitants from sleeping. And though for his part he had become accustomed to it, he did not wish to put me to so much discomfort. It seemed he had recently cast out a devil, or several, from an Augustinian nun, and the demons were avenging this deed. Despite these vexations, my brother had no fear of the devil whatsoever and would do battle with him at every opportunity. He used to say he feared himself more than the devil. One of his favorite sayings was "God save us from ourselves!" But as I have already mentioned in this account, the Revered Fray Juan was not exempt from temptations of the flesh. And he took great pains to see that they did not get the better of him. It was here that the devil set a snare for him after the matter of the Augustinian nun.

Naturally I did not heed his warning and stayed in the cottage. There were indeed noises in the night. But they did not trouble me.

"They are tiring of the game," my brother said, "for they know their endeavors are futile. As soon as they begin their din I start to recite my rosary and they are done for. I wonder what new villainy they have in store for me."

The new villainy, it seems, was to tempt him with a young woman of humble birth who was exceedingly beautiful. My brother used to say that earthly beauty was a reflection of Heavenly beauty, for which reason the devil found beauty more serviceable than ugliness. And although he was not much given to jesting, he would add: "In this at least the ugly ones have the advantage."

It was at about this time that a hermit appeared in Ávila. He claimed to be from the Holy Land. And indeed he looked like John the Baptist, with a rope around his waist, and he ate nothing but wild fruits and berries. Unbeknown to him perhaps (at least in the beginning), this man had received certain powers from the devil. Being a great deceiver, the devil delights in giving these powers to any who are willing to receive them, or care not whence they come.

Something of the kind happened to Saint Paul, when he was in Thyatira. One of his followers, a slave girl, had the gift of prophecy, which she used in order to procure money for her owners. This went on until the Apostle to the Gentiles cast an evil spirit out of her, so putting an end to the prophesying and the whole affair. As for the slave girl, all she would say, as she followed Paul and the others, was that they were the servants of Almighty God and that they were bringing word of the way to salvation. But Saint Paul grew weary of her tune and exorcised her, to the great displeasure of her owners.

The hermit, like this witch, was able to prophesy many things, among others that Fray Juan was a very saintly man. And he set about proving this in a haphazard fashion. He also claimed to be an admirer of the exalted form of prayer practiced by the Reformed Carmelites, and to be an exponent of it. Thus he became one of the first of the *alumbrados* in Castile, who claimed that only a soul united to God is whole. It was by this mystical route that the devil was able to lead him by the nose.

It seems he became acquainted with a young woman by the name of Lea, who was in the service of a rich merchant's wife in the city. Though she was simply the merchant's servant at first, she became somewhat more than this. Her mistress, greatly admiring her beauty, would show her off in rich attire, in the hope that some of the girl's beauty (for as I say she was exceedingly comely) would rub off on her. The hermit told the merchant's wife certain things that had happened in her life thus far. He also prophesied some event that came about. Consequently, she became very attached to him. The devil, however, finding little use for her because of her want of that which Lea had in abundance, used only the girl for his own purposes, namely, to set a trap for Fray

Juan. We know from the Bible that the devil is the father of lies, his artful practice to deceive this person and that. He had duped the hermit by allowing him to see certain things that others cannot. He also enabled the hermit to find water underground. This skill brought him considerable renown among the poor and those who tilled the land, for whom he would find wells. He also discovered a spring in a Carmelite convent. It was there that he learned about exalted prayer. He taught this to the lady. And between the two of them, they passed it on to Lea. And so unceasingly did they praise her beauty that by and by the poor girl came to believe it herself, it being most natural in woman to receive flattery with pleasure.

They were so taken with this "exalted prayer" that all three came to believe that she, Lea, had been given beauty for a purpose—so that she might conceive a child mystically and give birth to a new prophet. Maybe even Our Savior Jesus Christ, come again to right the evils of this world once and for all.

When the lady was delivered from the devil's clutches, she revealed all this and more in her deposition to the Holy Inquisition. But modesty forbids entering into details that have nothing to do with the part played in this business by the Revered Fray Juan. The intrigue deepened when the hermit decided that the man who was to get this beautiful girl with child must be an exceedingly saintly man. And he resolved that this should be none other than Fray Juan de la Cruz. Misguided as the hermit was, he profited by it, for he no longer had to eat roots and berries but had rich pickings from the table of the wealthy merchant, who was completely ignorant of the whole affair. He also profited from Lea, for under the pretext of instructing her in the matter of sublime union, he ended up possessing her. The lady too profited, as already mentioned. Believing Lea's beauty to predestine her for holiness, she reveled in the admiration of those who saw the respect shown her by a servant who was rumored to be a prophetess. So does the father of lies beguile the righteous.

The hermit saw to it that Lea lost no opportunity to cross my brother's path. She attended every sermon he preached at that time in the cathedral and other churches in the city. She was deeply impassioned by his beautiful words. And, but for the whisperings of Satan through the mouth of a hermit, and of her own mistress who had greater hopes for her than merely to be ravished by the words of a priest, she would have followed my brother down the path of righteousness.

The young woman's devotion had not escaped my brother's notice. She would stand near the pulpit, gazing upon him in rapt attention, and obliging him to avert his eyes, as he did with all women, especially beautiful ones.

Suffice it to say that between them all they turned the poor girl's wits. I can think of no other explanation for what happened next. One cold winter's night when the land was all in snow, I had gone out upon some errand or other. Thus my brother was alone when she knocked at the door of the little bothy in the garden, very scantily attired. Of what passed between them, all I know is this—my brother chided her gently but firmly; seeing this was to little or no avail, however, and the temptation severe, he opened a low casement nearby, picked up a handful of snow and threw it on his head. And he proceeded to cover himself in snow, as other saints have done in similar circumstances. Then, unshod as he was, he began to run, staying close to the hut. It was at this point that I returned. Lea was beside herself. I cloaked her in a blanket, and with the aid of the brother porter, a fellow of no mean strength, I conveyed her to the Augustinian convent. For the nuns there have some experience in such cases, which is to say of souls in turmoil, be it the work of the devil or through an infirmity of the wits. Fray Juan entreated us not to breathe a word of what had happened.

For he wanted to save souls that appeared to be lost. So it was in this case. For although Lea died shortly after this, she died in a state of grace. Her mistress repented before the Inquisition, laying open what I have here recounted. As for the hermit, he had to be put behind bars. And so he was. What his end was I do not know.

My brother learned much from this business. Afterward, he was considerably more alive to the stratagems employed by the devil with simple souls. For this reason he was very wary of beautiful objects, sweet smells, things that give delight to the touch and those that whisper to the senses, tempting the soul and leading it into sin. He called this "spiritual lust", from which it is but a short step to the other form. As to the events of that night, he said with humility that if it had happened in Córdoba, where it never snows, God alone knew how it would have ended. He also described the incident to his friars. And he warned them not to trust to their own strength but, in the absence of snow, to mortify their flesh with nettles. This was not the only occasion on which the devil tempted his baser passions. I could say a thing or two about the mistress of an inn in deepest Antequera. But not having been present, as in the case of which I have here given an account, I will leave it to those who can do so with greater authority.

For my part, I also learned much from that business, as always when I was with him. The days I spent with my brother passed in the twinkling of an eye. And he often had to remind me that my duty lay in Medina. Not only were my wife and children there but also our beloved mother, who had at last gotten over the fevers that racked her. And, by the grace of God, she was to be with us for another three years. Not that I had forgotten those dear to me, but my brother and I were so close that I found it hard to resist the pleasure of his company.

I also permitted myself this indulgence because I was

scarcely needed in the workshop, Eusebio the African having ensured that we were never short of work. And my wife
and mother were more than capable of attending to it, for
in the end they had six casual weavers in their employ.

Chapter 12

A Captive Poet

The devil's next move is more widely known. It was so subtle, in that it played on the conceited nature of the human soul, that it came within a hair's breadth of bringing down the Reform of the Carmelite Order.

As a contemporary historian observes, in order to understand what would otherwise be incomprehensible, a brief introduction is necessary. For how could brothers in the same Order have embarked on a fratricidal struggle that did untold damage to their immortal souls and was the scandal of Christendom, when the only difference between them was that some were shod and wore fine cloth while others were barefoot and wore rough serge?

In all this the individual who suffered most was Fray Juan de la Cruz.

As already mentioned, the father general of the Order, Juan Bautista Rubeo, was pleased with the Reform Mother Teresa had started. He encouraged her and gave her permission to found as many convents as she had hairs on her head. He was not so enthusiastic about the foundation of friaries, however. Alarmed by the belligerence of the Spanish Carmelite friars, he authorized only two, Duruelo and Pastrana. After considerable pressure from the prince of Eboli, one of Mother Teresa's most devoted supporters, Rubeo eventually agreed to the foundation of a third in Alcalá and, shortly afterward, a fourth in Altomira, Cuenca.

Philip II, however, was very much in favor of the reform of religious orders. He obtained permission from Rome to appoint apostolic commissioners with authority over the father general of the Carmelite Order. In 1569 two Dominican commissioners were appointed. Dominicans were chosen because of their reputation as theologians and rigorous monks. The first, Pedro Fernández, was given jurisdiction over Castile. The second, Francisco de Vargas, was given Andalusia.

Francisco de Vargas proved a somewhat incautious man. He was so in favor of the Carmelite Reform that he agreed to every request he received to found a house. He even went so far as to take the beautiful monastery in San Juan del Puerto, Huelva, from the Calced and give it to the Discalced Carmelites. Father Jerónimo Gracián de la Madre de Dios, a devoted follower of Mother Teresa and a frequent visitor to the province of Andalusia, was appointed prior. With the same enthusiasm he had always shown for the Teresian Reform, Gracián made life extremely uncomfortable for the Calced. Certainly the clerical hierarchy had been concerned about the lax nature of practices among the Calced, particularly when two monks were picked up in a brothel by the authorities. When Mother Teresa heard about this, she commented, "There is no cause for surprise in human frailty. We must simply repent and look to our own honor."

The Calced who still observed the mitigated rule were alarmed by what was happening. Believing it would bring down the secular branch of the Order, they formed themselves into a group and drew the attention of the father general, Juan Bautista Rubeo, to what was going on behind his back. Rubeo felt betrayed by Mother Teresa. Had he not always supported her? And was this how she now repaid him, by founding house after house without so much as a by-your-leave? Moreover, it was said that in some convents, she had permitted such extremes of penance that it was possible the devil was behind it, scheming as ever to bring down the whole Order. This kind of thinking was common among devout unreformed Carmelites and their supporters. These included some from the Carmelite monastery in Ávila, who coveted the position of vicar and chaplain of the Incarnation convent, a position held by Fray Juan de la Cruz. They knew very well that Mother Teresa had had nothing to do with these houses. But they also knew that if they could ruin Mother Teresa's reputation in the eyes of the father general, Fray Juan would fall with her.

Several irate letters from the father general to Mother Teresa demanding an explanation were intercepted. As she did not receive them, she did not reply. Had she done so, with her literary skill and the truth on her side, she would undoubtedly have set the record straight and things would have calmed down.

The Calced, interpreting Mother Teresa's silence as a stubborn refusal to cooperate, called a general chapter in Piacenza, Italy. And with a relish that bordered on spite, they revoked all the houses founded by the Discalced in Andalusia without the father general's permission. Furthermore, they forbade the foundation of any more houses, whether convents or friaries. Last but not least, Mother Teresa was confined to a convent.

Philip II, who had played such an important part in the foundation of the new houses, was informed of these decisions. Not wishing to become involved in a struggle between factions in a religious order, however, "the prudent king", as he was known, did nothing. The Calced took his silence as assent and went on the offensive. Accordingly, Mother Teresa was confined to the convent of San José.

As Ana de San Bartolomé was to comment:

> Nothing could have been more to her liking, no confinement sweeter. For as a consequence she did not have to receive visitors. This in turn enabled her to dedicate herself to communion with God, free from all the cares and obligations of the world—with one exception. She knew her beloved Fray Juan to be in grave peril. Such was our fear on that score indeed that in the end we became convinced he was dead.

When Fray Juan heard of these unprecedented events, especially Mother Teresa's confinement, he wrote her several letters full of Christian devotion and poetry.

"Most Revered Mother," he wrote,

> if there is anything I can do besides mortifying my flesh and praying for a swift end to the tempest and for all this business to turn out to be to the greater glory of God, you have but to name it.

"The greatest glory to God," she wrote in reply,

> would be for you to put as much distance between yourself and them as you can, for they are closing in on you as I write. This is no time for poetry.

Fray Juan immediately prepared to leave for the monastery of Altomira, Cuenca, the poorest and most enclosed house of the Reform. There he believed he could be unnoticed and unenvied. He was helped by the brother porter. Despite belonging to the Calced, he was deeply devoted to the saint. It was from this man that Fray Juan heard that some of his brothers coveted his chaplaincy and were plotting to take it from him.

"He had so few belongings, and they were so modest," the porter was later to testify,

> they could all be got into a single bag, and a small one at that. I suggested he hire a donkey for the journey, the cost of which doubtless some wealthy person in the city would lend him. He replied: "Why do you think God gave me legs, if not to use them? Is it not plainly written in the Gospels that Our Lord walked everywhere and that the only occasion on which He rode a donkey was to make His triumphant entrance into Jerusalem?" This was how the Revered Fray Juan used to speak. And that is why he walked at such a pace that few could keep up with him.

The worse things got between the Calced and the Discalced, the calmer Fray Juan seemed to become. If he was not in the confessional, attending the nuns of the Incarnation convent, he was in the countryside looking for birds and wild flowers. God had written such beautiful things in nature, he would say, that with the exception of the Bible, there was no book to match them. One day he was out walking with his friend and fellow Discalced brother Fray Germán de San Matías. Fray Germán's eyes filled with tears at Fray Juan's description of a rivulet skipping and bounding down the hill in search of the Adaja. When they came to a beautiful spot he would turn to Fray Germán and say, "Come, Father, let us give thanks to God."

He also experienced raptures. But when it was the confessional hour, or time for the divine office, he would come to himself, as if he had an internal hourglass. And he would go to perform his duties. He was very severe with friars who neglected their monastic duties because they claimed to be in a state of exalted prayer. He believed one of the purposes of purgatory was to bring us down to earth from prayer.

He felt a deep reverence for the blessed souls in purgatory. And he was rewarded with a vision of some ascending to Heaven like a ship coming into harbor on a gentle wind after a storm.

When he told the nuns of the Incarnation that he had decided to give up the chaplaincy and go to Altomira, there was general dismay and even some resentment.

"What sort of captain abandons his troops in the heat of battle?" asked the truculent prioress.

And one of the more moderate nuns said:

"You've done nothing wrong, Father. Yet you mean to slink away like a thief. Think how many souls you are helping to come nearer to God. Will you not be throwing away your just reward for the work of all those years if you go now?"

"I am not the arbiter of God's grace", he retorted angrily.

But it was nothing compared to the anger he felt that night when his door was locked from the outside, and the next morning when he was stripped of his habit. This effectively made him a prisoner. Even if he had been able to get out, he would have had to do so in his underwear.

The prioress immediately sent a message to one of her relatives at court, urgently requesting them to get word to the nuncio, who was lying ill in Salamanca at the time.

In her letter to the nuncio, she wrote, "This is not to be borne. I demand that Fray Juan be released immediately and confirmed as chaplain and vicar of La Encarnación."

Nuncio Ormaneto, who was in favor of the Reform, sent a messenger to Ávila without delay bearing confirmation of his agreement to this demand. Brandishing the nuncio's letter, the prioress said triumphantly, "Do you dare disobey the Holy Father in the shape of his representative in this court now, Father?"

Then, seeing his uncertainty, she added more gently:

"Do you not understand, Father, that we do this because of the great love we have for you through Jesus Christ Our Lord?"

"Mother Teresa has as much and more", he replied. "And she counsels me to leave."

This stung the prioress, who was not one of Mother Teresa's allies.

"Am I to understand", she said coldly, "that Your Reverence sets greater store by the words of a nun than those of His Holiness?"

"It seems to me, Reverend Mother, that the devil has more to do with this business than His Holiness. And if we are not careful, we shall all be tripped up by him. But if you order me to stay, then here I stay until they come and drag me away."

The prioress knew she had the upper hand. Disobeying an order from the papal nuncio was punishable by excommunication, and no friar, however recalcitrant, would be so foolish. Fray Juan believed Nuncio Ormaneto to be on his deathbed. And indeed, he died a few days later, on June 18, 1577, and was succeeded by Monsignor Sega, an implacable opponent of the Reform.

Seizing their opportunity, the convent's superiors tried to have Fray Juan locked up for insubordination. But the nuns called in some of the saint's devotees to guard him day and night.

The prioress was proud of this confrontation. Fray Juan remarked that she might have made a better soldier than a nun. Besides, what could armed guards do against the one who was behind the whole imbroglio?

His friend, Fray Germán de San Matías was later to comment:

Fray Juan wept at having to conduct his ministry under the
protection of Christian lances, as if in some heathen land.
He knew from the outset that it was all to no avail, for it was
inconceivable that Our Lord would permit such an absurd
situation to continue.

On this occasion, however, the powers of darkness got
the better of the powers of light. Word spread through the
city. There was to be no more talk about Fray Juan, or his
friends, or the nuns of La Encarnación. There were more
important things to think about. In the end, the guards were
removed. The time of year may also have been a factor in
this. As the saint's devoted guards kept up their vigil through
the bitter November nights, some of them began to wonder whether spring would ever come again. And some were
secretly relieved when the vigil was called off.

On December 2, 1577, a troop of armed men under orders
from the Calced marched to the bothy in the vegetable garden. They broke down the door and burst in, their harque-
buses leveled at Fray Juan and his companion, Fray Germán.

"So it begins", said Fray Juan calmly. "Welcome, gentlemen."

"Death to any who resists!" shouted the captain.

"I would not wish such a crime to weigh on your immortal soul for the world", Fray Juan gently assured him.
"I am ready. Do what you must."

Mother Ana María was keeping watch near the convent
gate. When she heard the noise, she went to see what all
the shouting was about.

She recounts:

He let himself be taken like a lamb. In spite of this they
dragged him out by the hair, disrespecting his person. Nor
did Fray Germán escape this usage. He also went meekly,

though presently he began to wriggle slightly. I did not show myself, for what could I have done against them? And so I hastened to return to the convent and made sure of the locks on all the doors, lest they turn their fury upon us.

Fray Juan and Fray Germán were arrested on the orders of the vicar general of the Carmelite Order, Father Jerónimo Tostado. He was Portuguese by birth, a doctor of theology from Paris, and a close friend of the father general of the Order. He had nothing against Fray Juan personally. He scarcely even knew him. But he was deeply suspicious of mysticism. He believed it led to *alumbrismo*, or *Illuminism*, which, as previously explained, frequently led to gross acts of carnality. This had been an obsession of his since his student days in Paris, where *alumbrismo* had been a serious problem. Nor did he approve of the reverence in which Fray Juan was held by the nuns. He did not think penitents should see their confessors as the only source of spiritual well-being. It might have surprised Father Tostado to know that Fray Juan agreed with this view. In fact, Fray Juan liked having another priest with him in case a penitent wanted a "second opinion".

It was for these reasons that "El Tostado", as he was known, opposed the Reform. The superiors of the Carmelite monastery in Ávila had told him that the way to crush the Reform once and for all was to break the will of Fray Juan de la Cruz, who, with Mother Teresa of Ávila, was generally considered to be its cofounder. This was true.

El Tostado chose Father Maldonado, prior of the Calced Carmelites of Toledo, to carry out the arrest of the two rebel friars from Ávila. Maldonado's first step was to have them flogged. The scourge was a common measure at that time for curbing pride. There was nothing arbitrary or irregular in this. Flogging was sanctioned in the rule of almost all religious orders. Friars were in favor of mortification of the flesh, whether self-inflicted or dealt out by superiors who knew what was good for their souls. But as the second series of lashes began, Fray Germán, who was younger and not so used to it as Fray Juan, cried out: "What have we done to deserve this punishment?"

Fray Juan, who was receiving the same treatment, replied: "And what did Our Lord Jesus Christ do to deserve this and much more? Let these good brothers get on with their work. For show me the sinner who would not gladly receive a little penance in this life if it shortened that in the next."

Fray Germán de Santo Matías died two years after this. By then the trouble in the Carmelite Order was over. He became prior of Mancera and was among those whom Fray Juan saw ascending directly to Heaven, as if on a cloth.

The saint was to comment, "I pray those trifling lashes old Tostado gave us in Ávila will do for me what they did for Fray Germán."

When the story of the events in the bothy broke, it caused quite a stir in the city of Ávila. Father Maldonado lost no time in setting off with Fray Juan for Toledo, where El Tostado the vicar general was waiting. Fray Germán, who was not as important as Fray Juan, was locked up in the monastery of San Pablo de la Moraleja near Arévalo.

Maldonado expected the saint's supporters to come after them. He had therefore hired some mules for the journey. At that time mules were normally reserved for clerical dignitaries and high-ranking civil servants. Fray Juan wondered why they should be conveying a prisoner like a bishop. They went by back roads, making long detours to escape notice. Whenever they passed through beautiful country, Fray Juan would become lost in mystical thought, as though in an ecstasy of prayer. His guards, many of whom were deeply envious of his position as vicar of the convent of the Incarnation, thought he was mocking them. It seemed to them that the fact that he was a prisoner accused of sedition could hardly have mattered less to him. They lashed him with tongue and whip. In response Fray Juan thanked them, which only increased their fury and the number of lashes they gave him.

The muleteer knew nothing about Calced or Discalced friars. But the meekness with which the prisoner took his punishment, and the beauty of his words, filled him with awe. When they stopped at an inn for the night, he offered to help Fray Juan escape. He would lead him over the mountains where the other friars would never find him. Fray Juan thanked the man for his offer. After considering it carefully, however, he turned it down. He still hoped that when he came face-to-face with Father Tostado, the celebrated theologian, he would be able to undo the harm done by a handful of impetuous Discalced friars. He was sure he could convince him that he was not rebellious and of how vital the Reform was.

Years later he was to say to his friars one Christmas Eve:

> Let us pray for a young muleteer who endeavored to help me some years since at about this time of year. Fool that I am, I did not know how to accept.

The year was almost over when they at last reached the Carmelite monastery of Toledo. The journey had taken a great deal out of Fray Juan. He was so thin that when he was stripped of his serge habit, a murmur went around the assembled friars. And when he was made to put on the habit of a Calced friar, some were moved to pity, others to laughter. He looked more like a ghost than a friar in the voluminous garment.

The monastery of Toledo was the Order's finest house in Castile. Standing proudly on the right bank of the Tagus in the shadow of the castle of San Servando, it looked more like a fortress than a friary. It was inhabited by some eighty friars living comfortably under the mitigated rule. Every single one of them was deeply opposed to the divisive shifts, as they saw them, of the reformers. Some of the younger members of the community were shocked by the whipping to which Juan was subjected. The older members, however, laughed at the idea that this half-dead-looking little friar should be trying to bring about a revolution in the Order.

Fray Juan never got the chance to put his case to the vicar general. El Tostado decided the best way to deal with these seditious reformist tendencies was to apply the letter of the law as defined by the chapter of Piacenza with the imprimatur of His Holiness Pope Gregory XIII. He accordingly convoked a canonical tribunal made up of like-minded members of the community, over which he himself presided.

At the hearing, Maldonado read out part of the edict of Piacenza. It stated:

> First, that those known as "the Discalced" have elected not to live in the monasteries of Castile as prescribed by the prior general is an undisputed fact. The same are, therefore, ipso facto, deemed to be rebellious.
>
> Second, the aforementioned Discalced have failed to take notice of and act upon with due humility the written orders of the prior general, by the use of specious arguments, excessive deliberation and prevarication.
>
> This being so, if the said Discalced fail to submit to the proper authority within three days hence, they will be subject to suspension *a divinis* and stripped of rank and right of reply and will be subject to other punishments deemed

necessary by their superiors, with recourse to the secular arm of the law, should it prove necessary.

Fray Juan's response was to the point: "I understand that Your Reverences must enforce the dictates of the chapter. However, it does not apply to me. For I am not among those who left their province to found houses in Andalusia."

After some whispered conferring among the members of the tribunal, the reply came.

"In our opinion, living in the dwelling in the vegetable garden of La Encarnación, which stands apart from the convent, is the same as leaving your province. Our judgment, therefore, is that you must now make a public admission of your guilt. If you agree, you will be reinstated to your proper position in the true Carmelite Order. This, incidentally, does not preclude the possibility of Your Reverence rising to the position of prior at some point."

Since further argument was clearly futile, Fray Juan replied: "If what Your Reverences seek applied to me alone, I would gladly give you satisfaction. But it is my unshakable belief that the Reform that lies at the heart of this is God's will. And on that I cannot give way. For I have vowed to serve the Reform to my dying day."

"Then death you shall have if you stand by this", thundered Father Maldonado.

The tribunal wasted no more time in pronouncing him "rebellious and contumacious". He was then sentenced under the rules of the Constitution. He was to be confined indefinitely at the discretion of the general of the Order. That night he was locked in the punishment cell. As the monastery was governed by the mitigated rule, the cell was comparatively luxurious. It had a good bed with a straw mattress, a table, a separate latrine, and a small window over-looking the garden through which the sound of running water could be heard. Had it not been for his anxiety about some of his brothers in the Order, the two months he spent here would have been among the most pleasant periods of his life. He was left completely alone to commune with God. He was allowed to attend Mass only on Sundays and holy days.

He requested confession. Even prisoners were entitled to this. The next day an ancient friar with a kindly face came to see him.

"My son," he began, "before I can hear your confession, you must renounce this foolish and damaging Reform. As soon as you do that, and agree to become a Calced friar again, you will be free to leave this dungeon. You will be given a new cell with its own library and a crucifix to wear around your neck like this one. Look, it is made of gold."

"He who stands naked before Our Savior Jesus Christ has no need of gold", the saint replied. "If I accepted Your Reverence's offer, I would be guilty in this respect. And in that case, I do not think Your Reverence would be the best confessor for me. God be with you."

With this, he turned his back on the old friar.

Within two months news came of the escape of Fray Germán de Santo Matía from the jail of San Pablo de la Moraleja. In the course of his escape, Fray Germán broke his leg. Fearing something similar, Father Maldonado ordered Fray Juan to be moved to a more secure place. He was put in a small cell measuring some six feet by twelve. The cell, which had no windows, only a high skylight, was normally the latrine of a cell used by journeying friars.

He was later to describe his time there:

What a good turn Fray Germán did me when he escaped. For the little cell I was moved to was built for humbler purposes. The hoary mists that rolled in from the river in winter made it so cold and damp that I lost many of my toenails and other parts of my body. And it was so close and airless in the heat of summer that I often gave myself up for dead. Suffice it to say it was a blessing when I was taken to the refectory to be given the rod, for it enabled me to fill my lungs with a breath or two of fresh air.

Fray Alonso the Asturian, compiler of the works of San Juan de la Cruz, was later to comment:

> The true blessing, however, lay in that thanks to the wretched conditions in which our Revered Father was held, his talent as a poet and writer was revealed. I do not say he had no talent prior to this. But whether because of the many tasks upon which he was engaged, or his natural modesty, this talent had not yet come out. Thus far, his writing (which was ever of the highest quality) had been confined to the business that fell to him as master of novices, or the little notes he was in the habit of giving his penitents. For the most part these contained some observation or other. Yet what were these compared to that which flowed from his pen within the confines of those narrow walls? Such exquisite verses that, but for his imprisonment, with nothing but the pen to comfort his soul, would doubtless never have come to light. O blessed confinement that once more proves the saying that God works in mysterious ways His wonders to perform!

This Heaven-sent period of imprisonment lasted some nine months. The treatment he received became progressively harsher as Father Maldonado carried out the instructions of his superior to the letter. El Tostado never doubted that he was acting as God's instrument to crush the Reform. Maldonado had been plagued by serious temptations since professing his vows in the Carmelite Order. It was only thanks to a superior, who subjected him to mortification of the flesh and imprisonment for several months, that he was able to rid himself of them and return to righteousness. Believing this to be good medicine for the rebellious soul, he administered it zealously and without mercy to the man his superiors had handed over to him.

Maldonado ordered the prisoner to be fed on bread and dried sardines. On Wednesdays and Fridays, according to the rules of the Constitution, he fasted. Friday was also the day on which he received communal punishment. He was taken from his cell and led to the refectory. Under the watchful eye of the prior and the community, he would kneel in the middle of the room to eat his food. The prior would again read out the charges against him and require him to consider the harm he was doing the ancient and holy institution of the Carmelite Order. If he failed to show any sign of contrition, he would be stripped to the waist. The prelate would start the whipping, followed by the rest of the community, until his back ran with blood. But no sound ever escaped the prisoner's lips. He accepted the punishment so meekly that some friars were unable to hide their distress. On one occasion a young friar who pitied him and barely touched him with the whip was rebuked by the prior.

"You do him no favors by sparing him what he deserves, Brother. Don't you understand that we are doing this not merely for the good of the Order but also for that of his immortal soul?"

"Obey your father prior", Fray Juan interjected. "There is no sin in obedience. And though my soul cries out against such usage, it does my body no harm to be reminded of its stupid condition."

Harsh though this treatment was, the saint bore the mental torture to which they subjected him less well. In the end he even came to doubt whether his actions were motivated by love of God, or mere obstinacy. The prior instructed the jailers to stage some whispered gossip about the Reform. They pretended the new nuncio, Monsignor Sega, had refused to have anything to do with the Discalced and that as a result the Reform had collapsed. In the end Fray Juan concluded it must be true. As the days and months wore on, he could think of no other explanation for why he had heard nothing from Mother Teresa. Unless she was in the same predicament as he . . .

Even more bewildering was how El Tostado had managed to keep where he was being held a secret from the whole country. In fact, El Tostado had forbidden every friar in Toledo to breathe a word about Fray Juan's whereabouts, threatening with excommunication anyone who talked. Meanwhile, Mother Teresa, who was confined to the convent of San José in Ávila, was worried to death about her beloved lost friar. She wrote several letters to Philip II demanding justice. She received no reply. But she thought Fray Juan might be in Toledo and asked the prioress of the convent of Discalced nuns there, Ana de los Ángeles, to see what she could find out. However, as her confessors, all of whom were Calced, were sworn to secrecy, she discovered nothing.

One night, which Fray Juan later called his "night of the Garden" [his Gethsemane], he came to the brink of despair. Forgotten by God and by his friends, he was on the point of sending for the prior to ask forgiveness and make a full confession of his guilt. Only one thing stopped him. Deep within him burned a tiny flame, his vow to be true to the Reform to his dying day. He decided to hold to this and let himself die. It would not be hard in his condition, consumed as he was by anemia and the suffocating heat, eaten alive by insects, his undergarments rotting away on his emaciated flesh. It was this above all that he found almost unendurable, having been fastidious about personal hygiene from an early age. Even in the depths of winter, if he came upon a stream, he would take the opportunity to wash himself and his undergarments. In the absence of a stream, he used any source of water he could find. If a friar neglected his personal hygiene to the point of stinking, he would take him aside and tell him that smells offensive to others were also offensive to God. At a time when people rarely washed (except for their feet), regarding it as something only Moors and heathens did, Fray Juan's love of cleanliness was remarkable. Nothing in his captivity distressed him more than not being able to keep himself clean, except maybe having to endure the stench of his own excrement in his tiny, airless cell for much of the day.

The night in question, his "night of the Garden", was a night of suffocating heat. Feeling that he was at the end of his endurance, he decided to refuse all food from then on. His daily ration was less than half a sardine. His death would satisfy those who saw his removal as the solution to the problems of the Carmelite Order.

He woke to feel a cooling sensation on his face. A young friar he did not recognize was mopping his brow with a damp cloth.

"Who told you to do this?" he inquired weakly.

"Must I be told to do what pity moves me to?" the young friar replied.

His name was Fray Juan de Santa María. He had just come from the Carmelite monastery of Valladolid. As a recent arrival to the community, he had been assigned to this duty by the prior. The duty was disliked by the other friars because it meant spending long hours in the underground chambers of the monastery with relatively few breaks.

Having received nothing but insults and abuse from his other jailers for some time, when Fray Juan heard the word pity, he was deeply moved.

"Do not trouble yourself, good brother", said the saint. "I will not burden you greatly, for I shall not be in this prison much longer."

Taking this to mean the prison of his body, the young friar replied, "That will not happen, if I can help it."

He wasted no time in bringing the saint some warm milk. He also gave him his leftovers from breakfast, which was considerably more nourishing than what the prisoner had received.

The following deposition by Fray Juan de Santa María appears in the cause for the beatification of the saint:

> I came from Valladolid, where the Discalced had no monastery. Consequently, though we had heard something of what had happened in Andalusia, and of the vexation this had caused our general, Father Rubeo, I knew next to nothing about the rebellion. When the Revered Fray Juan was entrusted to my care, I found him at death's door. Indeed, he was so weak and infirm that at first I thought him to be dead. Laying my hand on his brow, however, I found him to be alive. He was suffering from a high fever. I endeavored to bring some relief in the only remedy at my disposal, a little cool water. For this he could not have been more grateful had it come from the stream of Kidron itself. I also gave him a little milk, which he drank as if it were ambrosia. I never heard him utter the least murmur of complaint. From this I cannot but conclude that he experienced some raptures in that dark hole. Else it is beyond belief that he could have endured such suffering.

On Fridays it was my duty to take him to the refectory. While we sat down to eat, he knelt, eating nothing but bread and water. As soon as he had finished, the whipping began. His stripes, from which he bled profusely, took a long time to heal. One Friday when I had contrived not to take him down to the refectory, he said to me, "Brother, why have you spared me what I justly deserve?"

This I ignored. Whenever I could, I endeavored to keep him from the whip. One day he owned that he was not so distressed by the whipping as by his foul state. And he entreated me to give him some clean garments. I gave him one of our habits, there being no others in the monastery.

"Who would have thought", he joyously exclaimed, "that I would be so glad to put on the habit of a Calced Carmelite once more?"

Cleanliness was of the utmost importance to him. He seldom drank all his water but would use some of what little he was given to wash with. I was also struck by how much care he took to keep his lips clean. Indeed, he took such pains in this that he used the same napkin for weeks on end, for he left scarcely any mark upon it. Once, seeing me wipe my mouth on my sleeve after eating, he chided me, saying that this was an offense against poverty, for, serge or not, it did the habit no favors. For my part, though he had no authority to reprimand me, I gladly gave him ear.

One day, he asked me if I would be so good as to provide him with a little paper and ink. He said he wanted to set down one or two things of a devotional nature for his own amusement. If there was one thing that persuaded me of his sanctity, it was this. I can find no other explanation for how he came to write the sublime things he wrote in such wretched conditions. He wrote for himself and would not show me his work, saying it was worthless. But greatly desiring to see what he had written, I told him that as his jailer it was my duty to assure myself of his good intentions in writing. He replied it was only doggerel and that he had no skill for anything of greater worth. But he assured me the intention behind it was good enough. I spoke to him in this way not because I doubted his intentions, but to overcome his natural modesty. Thus I was able to compile what he wrote in that place, the "Cántico espiritual" (The Spiritual Canticle), "La fonte que mana y corre" (The welling and running spring ["For I Know Well the Spring"]) and "Las canciones de la noche oscura" (Songs of the dark night ["The Dark Night"]).

I have not the least doubt that enabling him to write was one of the best things I ever did. For had the prior known of it, he would unquestionably have forbidden it. But I kept my peace and furnished him with paper whenever he requested it, and a little bound notebook in which he wrote "La fonte". He made excellent use of the paper, writing on both sides and even in the margins. He also wrote in a minuscule, all-but-illegible hand. To do so he had to place himself directly under the skylight, which admitted scarcely any light at the best of times. On rare occasions, the sun coming out, a beam would pierce the gloom for a few brief moments. Then he would sit transfixed, as though drinking in all the power of Heaven in that beam of light. It was as if the Holy Spirit itself were illuminating him. And judging by what he wrote thereafter, I was not far wrong.

The first thing he read to me, though not the first thing he wrote, began thus:

> One dark night,
> Fired with love's urgent longings
> —Ah, the sheer grace!—
> I went out unseen,
> My house being all stilled.[1]

---

[1] "The Dark Night", stanza 1, in *The Collected Works of St. John of the Cross*, trans. Kieran Kavanaugh, O.C.D., and Otilio Rodriguez, O.C.D. (Washington, D.C.: ICS Publications, 1973), p. 711.

Though I did not understand them at the time, the words had a startling effect upon me. It was as though I had been run through by a hot blade. And though the words themselves conveyed much, how much more did the way he spoke them. Later he explained it to me. The dark night is when the soul, which is dying of mortification by all the things of this world, succeeds in shaking off this burden and comes to a life of sweet, nurturing love in God. To reach this point, the soul must undergo many labors and trials.

"Like those Your Reverence is going through in this place?" I ventured.

"Harsh as they are," he replied, "they are nothing to what I endure when Satan tempts me into pride."

He confided to me that the very night on which I became his guard, he had resolved to let himself die. And he said that in this there had been a measure of despair, which is born of rancor. And this in turn is wedded to pride.

We went on like this for three months or so. During this time I was more disciple than jailer. But except for his being able to write in secret, his lot did not improve. For the prior's orders did not change, nor did his meager rations. There was little I could do about this. Yet I did what I could, giving him some of my own food, though I had to entreat him to take it. One small favor I was able to permit him was the emptying of his latrine bucket. This we did at the siesta hour, when the community was at rest. We would go out to the cloister. And there I gave him leave to lean out of the great arches overlooking the Tagus. So it was that he discovered his whereabouts. And this in turn enabled him to plan his escape. Fray Juan must have inferred from this that if he had asked for my help to escape from that iniquitous jail, I would not have refused him. But he did not ask, and conceived his plan secretly so as to exculpate me in the eyes of my superiors. In this he did not succeed. For following his escape, as set down in our Constitution, I was stripped of voice and vote and made to sit in the lowest place in the refectory. But I was able to tell my superiors truly that I had known nothing about his escape plans.

Saddened as Fray Juan was by the harshness and incomprehension of his brothers in Carmel, I never heard a murmur of complaint from him on that score. He always found some way to excuse their actions and would not let me speak ill of them. He also told me that a good monk should accept the judgments of his superiors. And he exhorted me to do so. He was never bitter about what he had endured, and maintained that the Calced only acted as they did in the belief that it was the only way to achieve their ends.

The day he chose for his escape was the eighth day after the Assumption of the Blessed Virgin. On the eve, he begged me to forgive him for the trouble he had put me to. He also gave me a wooden crucifix with a bronze figure of Christ that he wore about his neck, where it hung next to his heart under his scapular. And he told me that it was to remind me of one who greatly revered the image of Christ on the Cross.

"Why", I asked in wonder, "do you wish to give me a thing of such great worth, Father?"

"As an image of Our Lord, it is indeed a thing of great worth", he replied. "But you have treated me as Christ Himself taught us to treat those who are the victims of injustice. And that is worth more."

From this, and the giving of such a gift, I had little difficulty in conjecturing what was about to happen. But I put it from my mind and placed the crucifix about my neck with deep reverence where it hangs to this day. And not for the world would I part with it.

Chapter 13

Like a Thief in the Night

On August 14, 1578, Fray Juan came to the decision to make his escape. It was the day on which he found out that the papal nuncio, Monsignor Sega, had overturned the instructions of his predecessor, Ormaneto, and given the Calced authority over the Discalced. Father Maldonado lost no time in communicating the news to his prisoner. He entered Fray Juan's cell and found him kneeling, his face turned up toward the skylight.

"Stand up when I enter your cell!" he shouted, kicking the saint.

"Forgive me, Reverend Father," Fray Juan replied, "I thought it was the jailer."

"What were you thinking about, so deep in contemplation?" Maldonado inquired irritably.

"That tomorrow is the feast of Our Lady, and what I would not give to celebrate Mass."

"Over my dead body", said Maldonado.

He followed this by telling the saint what Monsignor Sega had done. Distressing as this news was, Fray Juan was more distressed about not being able to celebrate Mass on such an important day. And if Father Maldonado had anything to do with it, it seemed he would have little chance of ever doing so again.

In contemporaneous accounts, Fray Juan's escape is described as miraculous. At any rate, the Blessed Virgin seems to have played a crucial part in it, appearing to him in dreams and telling him he must escape, and how to do it.

On this subject the saint comments:

> That I dreamed of Our Lady is true, though I endeavored to do so every night. In this I did not always succeed. It is also true that I commended myself to her, for I do nothing without first delivering myself into her hands. And that she helped me is no less certain, for what would have become of me without her help in this, as at every turn of my life, I do not know. In all other respects I conducted myself like one of those wretched creatures mentioned in the Gospels, the galley slaves, for I used every wile employed by them to escape their woeful plight.

The first thing he did was to measure the distance from the nearest window to the ground with a length of thread and a small stone. Then, as quietly as he could, he slid back the bolts on his cell door, which his kind jailer locked only at night. Last, he tore his blanket into strips and braided them into a rope.

The sixteenth of August, the day before his escape, he said good-bye to Fray Juan de Santa María and gave him the crucifix that Mother Teresa had given him. Though he treasured this, he valued his soul more. He knew what an appropriate and well-deserved gift it was. It was not wasted on him. In time, Fray Juan de Santa María professed his vows in the Discalced Order and made an excellent friar.

That night, as the moon rose, Fray Juan began his escape. He immediately ran into difficulties. To gain the balcony from which he would let himself down, he first had to pass through the adjoining chamber. As it happened, two journeying friars were spending the night there. It was a hot night. The friars were restless, tossing and turning, appearing to wake, then sinking again into fitful sleep. Fray Juan crept forward, then scuttled back again. He was in such a state of agitation that, as he himself put it, he forgot to commend himself to the Blessed Virgin.

But he gained the little balcony at last. Breathlessly he tied the rope to the guardrail. Undressing quickly to make himself as light as possible, he threw his habit into the darkness. He began to let himself down inch by inch. He did not know whether the rope he had made from old threadbare blankets would be strong enough. But his emaciated body weighed next to nothing, and the rope held.

It was only when he reached the ground, however, that his troubles really began. He found himself standing on a wall about three feet wide. He guessed this formed one side of the street. In fact, it was the wall of a courtyard of the convent of La Concepción. There he stood in nothing but his undershirt. His habit was nowhere to be seen.

As he was later to tell Mother Teresa in a letter:

Imagine the agony of anguish I underwent at the prospect of being discovered so attired in a place strictly out of bounds to any friar. The Calced were bound to retake me. And this time they would have ample grounds to treat me with even greater severity—not only because of my attempt to escape but because of the scandal of finding a friar in his undershirt in the hallowed precincts of a convent. In my desire for absolution I was seized by an urge to shout out a confession of my guilt, for I could see no way out of the courtyard. It was surrounded on all sides by buildings rising sheer to a height at which I could only guess. Before going any further, however, I commended myself to the patron saint of lost things, a saint whom I hold in the deepest reverence. Then, with infinite patience, I began to feel about in the shadows. And in that patience and in the virtue of this saint was my salvation, for I found the habit and, in so doing, the way out of that place. The habit had snagged on some protrusion and was hanging from a corner of the wall. How

it traveled so far in its fall, I cannot imagine. Unless it be
that my guardian angel conveyed it thither, so that in my
anxiety I might see that the wall was so rough hewn as to
afford me sufficient purchase to scale it. This I proceeded
to do. And on the other side was the street.

Fray Juan had never been to Toledo before. He had no idea
where he was. His only hope was to find the convent of
Discalced nuns. Its prioress, one of Mother Teresa's devotees, would help him to get out of the city. After so many
months as a prisoner, half-starved, his body weak from lack
of exercise, he knew he could not do so without help. It was
a warm night. The only people out and about at that time
were drunkards and prostitutes. In his bedraggled state, they
took him for an immoral friar and jeered at him. A pair of
prostitutes called out to him from a tavern and offered to
take him to their brothel for a blessing or two and a handful of *maravedíes*. Things went from bad to worse when he
ran into a group of fishwives. Taking him for a beggar or
a thief, they were about to stone him when a gentleman
intervened.

"In the name of God", he shouted, drawing his sword,
"why do you abuse this ruin of humanity thus?"

Fray Juan was later to remark, "Never was I more aptly
described. I have always been a ruin of humanity. Only it
was all the more obvious in my natural state, stripped of the
dignity that the habit confers on a monk or friar."

When he had driven away the angry gaggle of fishwives,
the gentleman warily surveyed Fray Juan. He concluded he
must be a leper, or something of the kind. Fray Juan knew
that if the dawn found him walking the streets, he was certain to be recaptured.

"Good sir," he said, "I am in need of lodging for the

night. My monastery is locked at this hour. If Your Honor will give me leave to sleep in your house tonight, though it be in the courtyard, I promise to be gone by first light."

"Monastery!" the gentleman exclaimed. "What kind of monastery is there for the likes of you?"

Fray Juan swayed and sank to his knees.

"I humbly beseech Your Honor. . .", he said faintly.

"Very well", said the gentleman quickly.

And he told Fray Juan that he could spend what was left of the night in his entrance hall. Fortunately for Fray Juan, the gentleman's house, a Toledan town house with a coat of arms over the door, was nearby. But he told his servant to lock both the main door and the door to the inner courtyard.

There was nothing in the entrance hall but a stone bench. Giving thanks to God, Fray Juan lay down on it and instantly fell into a deep and untroubled sleep. This was only partly because he was so exhausted. Something told him that he had been right to escape, if only for the sake of the Reform.

The next morning, the servant came to let Fray Juan out. Warily he pushed some bread across the floor toward the saint. Like his master, the man assumed the disheveled little friar to be a leper. Fray Juan thanked him and asked him for directions to the convent of Discalced nuns.

"You have but to go out onto the street", the servant replied. "It is next door. But I must warn you that it is a closed order. They have no dealings with the likes of you."

"Praise God!" the saint exclaimed. He had been afraid he would have to walk the streets in full daylight with the Calced hunting him high and low.

Fray Juan knew there was no time to lose. He immediately went out onto the street and knocked at the *torno* (the turn, a revolving cupboard) of the convent. At length a small panel in the *torno* opened. The *tornera* [turn sister] regarded the saint in silence.

"Sister," Fray Juan began, looking anxiously up and down the street, "let me in, I pray you."

Eyeing him dubiously, the *tornera* said:

"The Hospital for Infectious Diseases is not far from here. It is run by the *mercederas*. They will look after you."

"Sister," he implored, "I am Fray Juan de la Cruz. This night I have escaped. Go. Tell your mother superior. Quickly, I beseech you!"

The panel slammed shut. The saint heard the nun's footsteps shuffling slowly away. He looked up and down the street, dreading that at any moment, he would be seen and captured. They were sure to know that he had escaped by now. The streets were already filling with people. Some passersby stared at him, a bearded, long-haired ghost of a friar in a tattered habit without cape or cowl, hanging around outside the convent.

After what felt like an eternity, he heard footsteps returning. There was a jangle of keys. A lock turned and the little panel in the *torno* opened to reveal the prioress, Ana de los Ángeles, and the two key-holding sisters. Fray Juan was not surprised to see their blank looks. They did not recognize him.

"Reverend Mother," he said urgently, "it is I, Fray Juan de la Cruz. Let me in, for the love of God."

They recognized him as soon as he opened his mouth. But they were so distressed at the sight of him that they were lost for words.

"Sisters," Fray Juan said with mounting desperation, "your tears will not help me. The first place the Calced will look is here. If they find me, I am done for. Yet I think Our Lord has other plans for me."

"Open up, Sisters", said the prioress, finally grasping the seriousness of the situation.

Not until he heard the sound of the three bolts sliding shut on the only door that communicated with the outside world again did Fray Juan breathe a sigh of relief.

Less than two minutes later, a pair of Calced friars with a constable knocked at the *torno*. They asked the *tornera* if she had recently let in a fugitive. Her evasive replies made them suspicious, and they searched the parlor and the adjoining church. But they did not dare force their way into the enclosed part of the convent. This was strictly forbidden by their Constitution.

At midday the nuns brought Fray Juan some pears stewed in wine and cinnamon.

"I never tasted anything so delicious", he said as he devoured the pears.

He had drunk no wine in a long time, and it went straight to his head. To the astonishment and delight of the nuns who clustered around him, he suddenly launched into a fervent recitation of his "Spiritual Canticle". The sister cook, Teresa de la Concepción, brought him another dish of pears in the evening. But he declined, saying it would be greedy to eat any more.

That night a canon of the cathedral by the name of Don Pedro de Mendoza came to the convent, of which he had long been a benefactor. He offered the saint the protection of his house until he was well enough to undertake a journey. It so happened that this noble prebendary's house stood next to the Carmelite monastery in which Fray Juan had been imprisoned. Through the slats of a shutter in an upstairs window, Fray Juan watched the comings and goings of the Calced. They were often accompanied by constables, presumably searching for him. And he thanked God that despite his being under their very noses, they could not find him.

He was to remain in this house for two months. This was partly because of his health, partly to allow the hunt to subside. One day Don Pedro, who was also an administrator of the Hospital de Santa Cruz, brought a trusted surgeon of Moorish descent to examine him. The surgeon was amazed that a person who appeared to have no blood in his veins should still be alive.

Don Pedro's deposition also appears in the cause for beatification. In this he states:

> The *chirurgeon*, who, although a *morisco* [Moorish convert], was an illustrious physician, confided to me that my charge was at death's door and had been so for some time. Grievous harm had been done to him. When I told the Venerable Fray Juan of this, he replied that those who have yet to fulfill their obligations to Our Lord Jesus Christ do not die. And he said he still had some work to do before going to meet his Maker. Nor did he die then, though there were times when I thought he was on the point of doing so. The dried sardines he had been fed on in prison had rotted his stomach and made him bilious. There were times when he could not even keep down milk, only some stewed pears that were sent from the convent. Yet despite his infirmity, he was never too sick or too tired to pick up his pen and work on some verses he had written in prison, going over them again and again until he was satisfied. Of these I can recall "The Spiritual Canticle" and "The Dark Night", which I would often read in the evening to the mutual benefit of our souls. If there is anything on which I can fault him it is in this, that now and then, he stood a little in want of modesty as to his skill as a poet. But he would presently become sensible of it and repent, on occasion to excess. Once he went so far as to fear that it was all vain and foolish

nonsense and told me he had a good mind to tear it up. I replied that if he did, I would give him up to the Calced so that they might teach him humility and truthfulness. He obeyed me. Nor could he have done otherwise, for during that time I was his confessor, there being no other. And without breaching the confidentiality of the confessional, I can divulge that no monastery ever surpassed the devotion that reigned in my house during those months. Besides the coachmen and grooms, my household consisted of a pair of maidservants, a doorkeeper and her niece, and another two or three servants. Some of them knew who my guest was. Others did not. But none of them would have denounced him—not out of respect for me, but because of the devotion he inspired in them. We celebrated Mass in a small oratory in the west wing. And when it fell to Fray Juan to officiate, my servants would quarrel about whose turn it was to attend, whereas if I was the celebrant, I had to remind them that it was Sunday or a feast day. He confided to me that during his imprisonment he had felt the deprivation of the Eucharist more keenly than that of food and that the Consecration was now attended by many special favors from the Lord. On one occasion, as he raised the Host, we saw him rise a little way off the ground. But he denied this, saying that we had imagined it and that on no account were we to speak of it.

When he heard that the troubled waters between the Calced and the Discalced were calm once more, he told me it was time to go. He set off for Almodóbar, where a chapter had been convoked for the month of October of the same year, 1578. I did my best to persuade him to stay, his health as yet being only slightly improved. He replied that his only reason for doing something as unseemly as to escape from prison by sliding down a rope had been so that he might play his part in the Reform of the Order. In view of this, he could not in good conscience pass up such an opportunity. I felt his departure keenly. And, but for my advanced years and the attractions of a life of ease, to which I had become too accustomed, I would have followed him.

Chapter 14

In Southern Parts

The bitter feud that so nearly derailed the Reform was to go on for another two years. Finally, however, on June 22, 1580, Pope Gregory XIII authorized the division of the Calced and the Discalced branches of the Carmelite Order into separate provinces. This had long been the dream of Fray Juan de la Cruz. It had also been that of Mother Teresa. She knew it was achieved principally through the intercession of Philip II, to whom she had written letter after letter during her confinement in the convent of San José in Ávila.

In his account to Father Velasco, Francisco de Yepes alludes to this as follows:

That La Madre wrote His Majesty many letters is beyond dispute. But he received many more with widely differing views, for she was not alone in being able to write. And there were many among the Calced with friends in high places. It was at about this time that Eusebio Latino, the African slave whom our father befriended, returned to Medina. Naturally we told him of the imprisonment of my brother, though we knew little or nothing about it. When we heard some months later that my brother had escaped, we were surprised to have received no word from him. But we put it down to the many enterprises he was working on. Scarcely anything was known in Medina about the struggle between the Calced and the Discalced. And even if we had

known anything, it would not have occurred to us that my
brother was involved in it, for he had always believed in love
among all Christians. As soon as we heard that he had been
arrested, I went to Ávila to speak to La Madre in person. I
found her in good health, though considerably aged. In view
of what she had endured, however, this was not surprising.
She told me of the anguish my brother's imprisonment had
caused her, for she loved him as much as we did, if not more.
And she told me that she had written many letters to the
king complaining of the great injustice of imprisoning so
saintly a man and that it was not to be borne, repeating this
message again and again. And she told me she had written
to other people at court, entreating them to intercede with
the king on her behalf.

On my return to Medina, somewhat though not entirely
reassured, I met Eusebio Latino, who always visited us whenever he passed through Castile. On this occasion he was overjoyed to be returning home from England, where he had
been lecturing in grammar at one of those universities so
admired by humanists. His beard (which it is not given to
all Africans to have) was full and silvered, as was his hair,
which gave him a distinguished air. He was tall, his bearing
still erect, and though by no means portly, he was an imposing figure. His attire was rich in the extreme. Anyone
who saw him on the street, whether on foot or in a coach
attended by servants, would undoubtedly have taken him for
the ambassador of some distant land. No one would ever
have imagined that he had once been the slave of a family
of weavers.

The news of my brother's arrest troubled him deeply. And
he reproached us for not acquainting him with it sooner,
so that he might see what he could do. This, as we were
soon to learn, was a great deal. He had met Fray Juan only
some three or four times, as I recall. Yet he commended him
ceaselessly for the qualities he discerned in him. Like father,
like son, he would say. But he also said that though he bore

little or no outward resemblance to our father, in his soul he was the very image of him, only more exalted. Given the exceedingly high esteem in which Eusebio Latino still held our father, his regard for my brother was remarkable. He also gave my brother money for the foundation of his houses, but secretly. Some years after Fray Juan had regained his liberty, deeply revered in Andalusia, (I forget now whether it was in Beas or Manchuela in the province of Jaén), he found himself in need of money. Then, quite unexpectedly, he received a donation from an unknown source, which got him out of difficulties. No one, not even my brother, knew who the benefactor was. He wasted little time pondering the matter, however, having great faith in Providence, which never forsook him. He used to tell his friars that instead of going from house to house begging for alms, they would be better served staying in their own cells and telling Our Lord what they wanted, for He was sure to answer their every need.

The year 1584 was one of great hardship. The rains failed and there was widespread famine in Andalusia. It affected not only the poor but the artisans and even the nobility. Yet my brother, who was then prior of the monastery of the Holy Martyrs (convento de los Mártires) in Granada, ordered that no one should be turned away unfed. As a result there was a constant stream of people at the doors of the monastery begging for food. The friars could not understand how Fray Juan had so much food to give out when the monastery was so poor. It seemed to them like the feeding of the five thousand. Thanks to anonymous donations, not once did the monastery of the Holy Martyrs run out of grain that year. But as I was later to discover, the donation to Beas or Manchuela was certainly from Eusebio Latino.

Returning to the matter of Fray Juan's arrest, Eusebio Latino, who was then private secretary to an eminent government official (I believe the minister for taxes), began to circulate Mother Teresa's letters. It seems these generated such a great deal of files and documents that they could have filled a cart and bogged it in the mire. His triumph lay in that he "pulled the cart out of the mire". For he succeeded in speaking to one of the king's most trusted councillors, the Conde de Tendilla. Thus the matter came before the royal council at last, whereupon the king ordered the appointment of three Dominican commissioners to conduct an inquiry into the dispute in the Carmelite Order. The result of this was a proclamation that the Discalced should be set free from the jurisdiction of the Calced, thus putting an end to many evils. Eusebio was beside himself with joy, as were we.

The fact that Fray Juan's movements were no longer constrained by the Calced greatly assisted the progress of the Reform. It was also of much comfort to our mother, for it enabled him to be with her when she breathed her last. She died of the great fever of 1580. My wife and I also fell sick of this fever, but being younger and stronger, we were able to make a good recovery. Not so our mother, however. She was well on in years by then and had become increasingly susceptible to little fevers, until the great fever of 1580 carried her off. Fray Juan was in Andalusia at the time, founding the school at Baeza. As soon as he got word of her condition he came away, asking for help from a wealthy gentleman, who lent him a horse so that he might journey to Medina with all speed. This was one of the few occasions in his life when he did something like this. Although this fever had also spread to the Baeza school, it did not prevent his coming, for he placed our mother higher in the scheme of things than his brothers in Carmel.

He arrived one night and our mother died on the morrow. It was as though she had been waiting for her beloved son. Over her last days she barely had the strength to fetch her breath. No sooner did she set eyes on him however, than the tension in her features ebbed away and her visage filled with joy. She could not say more than a few words. But what she did say before she breathed her last meant all the world to us. What Fray Juan said to her was also of great beauty. My wife and I, and one or two neighbors who were with us to help her in her hour of death, were all enraptured. When she died, we all fell to weeping with grief. Yet Fray Juan stood very still by her side. And when I looked into his eyes I saw they were dry.

"Why do you not weep, brother?" I said through my tears. "Would it not comfort your soul?"

"Why would I weep when I have just seen her going up to Heaven?" he replied.

He was very sure of this. Indeed, the only reason he allowed us to hold a funeral was so as not to give rise to idle talk, for she had no need of one. I was struck by the vision of which he had spoken. And I could not help asking him what Heaven was like.

To this he did not reply, either then or subsequently. He did speak about hell, but of Heaven he would not speak. It was the same with La Madre, who once had a terrifying vision of hell. But of Heaven she would say nothing. She also fell ill of the great fever and nearly died of it. Our Lord prevented it, however, for He still had some work for her to do. All I can say is that on no account would Eusebio Latino permit us to tell La Madre of the part he had played in furthering her petitions. He did not want her to hold herself in lesser esteem because she had been unable to do what an African had succeeded in doing. In this he showed how little he knew Mother Teresa, for when she did find out, she laughed, rejoicing in the fact.

As I say, neither La Madre nor my brother presumed to speak of Heaven, it being a thing so ineffable that they could find no words for it. And it is said that something of the kind befell Saint Thomas Aquinas. After a lifetime attempting to explain God, he had a vision of God that rendered him so speechless that all he could say about his great work was that it was straw.

As we already mentioned, Francisco's confessor, Father Velasco, regarded his penitent to be almost as saintly as his more famous brother. Velasco wanted him to write an account of his own life. Francisco was an old man with failing vision by then, and Velasco appointed three secretaries to help him. The most scholarly of these was Francisco de la Peña. When the narrative reached the point of Catalina's death, de la Peña wrote to Father Velasco, who was then in Segovia.

"As Your Reverence knows," he wrote,

> the work upon which I am engaged is to be entitled *Life and Virtues of the Venerable Man Francisco de Yepes*. It is to be published posthumously to spare the author's modesty. Given that he is clearly disposed to say increasingly less about himself and to concentrate almost exclusively on his brother, should we not change the title?

Father Velasco replied:

> Agreed. Use your own discretion as to the title. Be as concise as possible in describing what remains of the life of Fray Juan de la Cruz. Confine yourself to occasions on which Francisco was present or had eyewitness accounts of what took place.

Francisco de la Peña did as instructed. The book was published in 1617 under the title *Life and Virtues of the Venerable Francisco de Yepes, Who Died in Medina del Campo in the Year 1607: Containing Many Things of Note about the Life and Miraculous Works of His Saintly Brother, Father John of the Cross*.

What Francisco de la Peña considered worthy of inclusion in this account is as follows:

I never missed an opportunity to visit my brother. And to this my wife did not object, seeing how much my soul benefited from these visits. There were also several occasions on which we sought his advice. One such was when our eldest daughter, Ana, decided to give herself to Our Lord Jesus Christ in a religious life. Naturally we were overjoyed. And we took it for granted that it would be in Carmel, because of our great love for the Order. What was our dismay, then, when she told us that although she wished to enter religious life, it would not necessarily be in Carmel.

I immediately made preparations to go to Granada, where Fray Juan was a greatly revered prior. Thus I took a coach and, going by way of Madrid, reached Granada a few days later. There was more than enough money for this, for thanks to Eusebio Latino's generosity, we had been able to put a little by. Not that he gave us money, but much work so that we might want for nothing, which is better. When my brother saw me arrive in a coach, he made some wry comment or other about the ease to which I had grown accustomed. But he did not think it improper; unlike him, I had taken no vows of poverty. As I soon discovered, these were extreme. On the day I arrived, he asked the lay brother cook to serve a guest's dinner. This consisted of some stewed nettles and chickpeas and a young wine that they had made themselves, though it was not wine-growing country.

"If this is a dinner reserved for guests," I said to the lay brother when we were alone, "what is an ordinary one?"

"Any young herbs or grasses growing in the fields, so long as they are not poisonous. With these, and some pork belly if we have any, we make a simple stew", he replied.

"Praise God you do not also eat the poisonous ones", I said, only half in jest.

"Have no fear", the man earnestly replied. "We pick only what our donkey grazes on. But so long as it is not poisonous we make use of whatever we find."

And he went on to explain that during the foundation

of the Calvario house in the Sierra de Segura, they had observed that the animal grazed only on certain grasses known as *jamargos*. And they had found that if turned out onto a board when half-cooked, pounded and returned to the pot, they were less bitter. I had words with my brother about this, for I could not see the need for such rigor. He replied that he could. For it seemed some of his friars had only to acquire a few possessions to forget that they were still as bound to poverty as when they owned nothing. Nevertheless, as his elder brother, I felt it my duty to take him to task. He, meanwhile, broached the subject of my reason for coming, namely, my daughter's vows. He told me that on no account was I to insist that she profess these in Carmel. For a vocation is not given by parents but by God. Of this he was deeply convinced. And I thank God that I had made the journey, for my daughter ended up professing in the convent of the Bernardas del Sancti Spiritus, in Olmedo, where she lives in perfect contentment to this day.

He was working on *The Ascent of Mount Carmel* at the time. He had begun this while at the monastery of Calvario, Jaén. In his heart he yearned to write. And on occasion, as he wrote, I had the rare privilege of witnessing a kind of radiance about him, as though the Holy Spirit were guiding his hand. But he was also mortifying his flesh a good deal in respect of this. On no account would he write if he had some duty to perform, particularly if it was to do with the care of souls. For he believed the soul of the lowliest person to be worth more than all his writing put together. He would occasionally say he would write no more. But his confessor forbade him to stop. And although my brother was the prior, he had taken a vow of obedience. Besides, I do not believe he would have been able to stop, for to lock up within himself what must perforce come out would have been like burning his own entrails.

We went into the country almost every day. And when he saw some trifling thing or other, he would point it out and set it down in a little book he carried about with him. On one occasion he took us to a place at the confluence of the Genil and the Darro, from where the snow-capped sierra could clearly be seen. Here he saw some little fish and called out joyfully: "Come, Brothers, see how God's little creatures praise Him!"

We looked, but were not so transported as he. Sometimes on these walks we found him hovering a foot or so above the ground. His friars were so accustomed to these raptures that they scarcely even noticed them. When he came to himself again, he would take out his little book and begin to write. He also wrote many little notes to the nuns who flocked to him. He gave fewer to his friars, however, as he had more opportunities to speak to them in person.

There was a pleasing incident at about that time touching on the admission of a postulant. Fray Juan had advised the community not to accept him. The fellow was already well into middle age. And though he appeared quite prosperous, he was offering to do the more menial work like the humblest of lay brothers if they would only admit him to the Order. The master of novices supported him, praising the fellow to the heavens for his piety. Not wishing to undermine the master of novices, Fray Juan consented, but cautioned them not to be in too much haste to fit him for his habit. A few days later the postulant's wife and children turned up at the gates of the monastery looking for him. This amused some, though not all. Of these the master of novices was the least amused. Indeed, he was all for turning the fellow over to the magistrate for abandoning his family. But Fray Juan took it upon himself as prior to talk to the man. He asked him whether instead of carrying out the lowliest work in the monastery he would not be better off embracing the noble task of being a good husband and father, for it was there that he would find God. My brother was not in the habit of saying things in jest. But in this case he remarked to his friars that their life was evidently no great sacrifice, since there were some who would prefer it to providing for a wife and children. The man's wife turned out to be a peevish woman. Thus he also spoke to her, in the hope that she would treat her husband better, lest he run away from her again.

The incident was pleasing because it ended well. For the man became one of Fray Juan's penitents, and being a well-to-do farmer, he would bring sacks of wheat to the monastery. I believe he was among those who helped the community most during the famine of 1584.

There was another incident to do with a young man. This one, however, was somewhat less felicitous. For the young man set fire to a convent in Salamanca in an extremity of unrequited love when his beloved professed her vows in it. Pursued by officers of the law, he ended up at the monastery of which my brother was then prior and begged for sanctuary.

My brother asked the fellow, "Why do you seek sanctuary? Is it to save your body from the punishment it merits, or to save your soul from the torment of hell?"

He would say things of this nature, things that spoke to the souls of others, as on this occasion. For when this hothead, Francisco Enríquez de Paz by name, at last comprehended the enormity of what he had done, he greatly desired to atone for it. Fray Juan told him he must first make good the damage he had done—(the burning down of a wing of the convent, which, by the grace of God, had not led to loss of life). This he did by selling some land he owned near Arévalo and sending the money to the nuns in Salamanca. The matter did not rest there, however. The young man had been denounced to the Inquisition, which had accused him of desecrating a holy place. This heretical act was a capital offense. Fray Juan defended him, arguing that a wing, though part of a convent, was not a sacred place. Furthermore, the cause of his action had been unrequited love, which is not a religious offense. Fearing the worst, however, the young man would not leave the monastery in case he was arrested, and there he stayed for years. My brother did not bar the young man from any acts of the community save the monastic chapter, and I came to know him myself.

There is no end of stories like this about my brother's deeds. He valued the care of souls more highly than the writing of things of beauty. Yet he did not stop writing. In Granada, at the behest of Doña Ana de Peñalosa, widow of Don Juan de Guevara, he wrote "The Living Flame of Love", which is very dear to me. This Segovian lady was exceedingly wealthy. Thus she agreed to my brother's request to leave some of her money for the building of the convent of Discalced nuns in Segovia. In return he agreed to write something for her. He wrote "The Living Flame of Love" while I was in Granada. When it was done—I remember it well—a servant of Doña Ana's came to collect it. Fray Juan was about to give it to the servant when his confessor hurried in and said that on no account was he to do so.

"Why not?" Fray Juan asked. "I wrote it for her."

But the father confessor placed such a high value on my brother's writing that he would not consent to its being taken away. He made the servant copy the manuscript. This took him several days. Had it been up to this confessor, he would have had copies made of every note and letter he wrote. And had he done so, they would not have been lost to posterity, as so many of them now are.

In Granada I witnessed the deference he showed to devout and wealthy ladies such as Doña Ana de Peñalosa. Yet he treated others who were far less qualitied than she with the same deference. I recall in particular two mulatto women, Isabel and Emeteria by name, who came to him for confession. Both of these women were the property of unscrupulous masters who abused them.

He had no fear of sin. He would often say that the only thing we had to fear was not fearing being sinners. On one occasion we were journeying in the region of Alcolea, on the Guadalquivir River, accompanied by brother Martín de la Asunción and two lay gentlemen. We had stopped at an inn on a bend of the river in the Vegas Cordobesas when we were approached by a prostitute. As soon as she set eyes on us, she began to make lewd gestures, as those in that sad trade are wont to do, not having noticed perhaps that some of our party were religious. One of the gentlemen picked up a stick and was about to beat her, doubtless thinking of the offense it might cause my brother. But my brother stopped him. And turning to the unfortunate woman, he chided her and reminded her that Our Lord Jesus Christ had redeemed her soul with His blood. No sooner had he spoken these words than the woman fell senseless to the ground. There she lay for some time. And when she recovered, she smote the air with her cries for confession. Fray Juan comforted her with wise words and sent her with a letter to the Discalced convent in Córdoba, where she would be taken care of. Some time later (I did not see this but have it on good authority), she married in that city and led a virtuous life [as a tertiary] clothed in the habit of Saint Francis.

I say he had no fear of sin precisely because he did fear it. He did not trust himself but always commended himself to Our Lady of Mount Carmel. There were a number of women who endeavored to ensnare him with temptations of the flesh. But he took no offense and reminded us of the words of Saint Augustine—that there is no sin or crime that, for all our frailty, we could not have avoided committing. And that if we had avoided it, the only reason was that God in His infinite mercy had prevented us from committing it and delivered us from evil.

This is all I can recall of importance about the Venerable Fray Juan during those years.

Chapter 15

Where There Is a Want of Love

Fray Juan wandered placidly through Andalusia, giving rise to prodigious events wherever he went. He carried out his superiors' orders, founding houses in Manchuela in the province of Jaén, and in Caravaca, Murcia. He also had to accept the priorate of Segovia in the house endowed by Doña Ana de Peñalosa. Had it been up to him, he would certainly have led a more secluded life, following his contemplative inclinations.

A papal brief issued by Sixtus V in 1587 saw the formation of a committee known as the Consulta. The Consulta was to govern the Discalced Carmelite Order. Fray Juan was third councillor on this committee. Finding the work tedious, he was not given much to do. He did what he was asked to do, however, because, as one of the founding reformers, he wanted to keep the spirit of the Reform going. In the course of his work on the Consulta, he ran into a number of problems that he was able to turn to his advantage to smooth his path to the Kingdom of Heaven.

The vicar general Father Doria called an extraordinary session of the Consulta in Madrid in 1590. The saint had always obeyed Father Doria to the letter. But in matters of judgment he tended to be guided by his own moral sense and the founding zeal he had shared with the late Mother Teresa.

At this session Father Doria proposed that the nuns of the Discalced Order be placed under the jurisdiction of the Consulta. But the nuns did not want this. The only function of the Consulta, in their view, was to bungle and prolong the decision-making process. To the annoyance of the vicar general, Fray Juan agreed. Father Doria's annoyance only increased when the nuns enlisted the help of their friends and relatives and appealed directly to the Pope. Instead of being governed by the Consulta, they wanted to appoint a commissioner from among the Discalced prelates. And they wanted this to be Fray Juan de la Cruz, who was prior of the monastery in Segovia at the time. When the Holy Father agreed to their request, they lost no time in communicating the offer to Fray Juan. With his knowledge of human nature, his experience of the mess rational people can get themselves into and the devil's influence in such things, however, he knew it would only lead to trouble. And he declined.

"Sisters," he wrote,

> your love for me would do me no favors. I believe it would be used as a pretext to banish me to some distant corner. In any case I am certain it would be disallowed.

The nuns were bitterly disappointed. Some were even irritated by his lack of fight and assured him that all the world liked and loved him.

"In that case," he replied,

> I would certainly have failed, for Our Lord, who never failed in anything, died on the Cross for those who did not love Him. And in this, if in nothing else, I would emulate Him.

Fray Juan was not proud of having enemies, many of whom were among his own kind. Most notable of these was a brilliant young preacher by the name of Father Evangelista, whom he had censured for vainglory in the pulpit on a visit to Andalusia. He had also told him that he was spending too long away from his monastery on his many preaching engagements. Evangelista was not the only priest whom Fray Juan censured. But he was certainly the one he most egregiously offended in so doing. Diego Evangelista, a favorite of Father Doria's, was appointed councillor general at the general chapter of 1591 in Madrid. Almost the first thing he did was to relieve Fray Juan of his responsibilities. If Fray Juan was no longer a prelate, he could not hold the position of commissioner of Discalced nuns. And to prevent any protest or scheming to that end, he proposed to send Fray Juan to the New World. A small band of friars was about to undertake the conversion of a land that, having suffered under the yoke of the Aztec empire for centuries, was now offering itself to Christ with open arms. And the man they had requested to lead them in this monumental task was Fray Juan. The land was called Mexico.

"Nothing could be more to my liking", Fray Juan replied, overcome by emotion. "I will gladly do this, if it please God to grant me sufficient strength for it."

At the same chapter on June 25, 1591, an order was drawn up for the departure for Mexico of a dozen friars led by Fray Juan de la Cruz. He was to go immediately to the place nearest to their port of embarkation in Andalusia. Not surprisingly, the nuns protested. The prioress of the convent of Segovia, María de la Encarnación, was the loudest of these. With connections at court, she spoke out publicly against the decision, vowing she would walk barefoot to Rome and protest to the Pope if necessary. The saint, knowing her character, wrote to her. He begged her to do no such thing and forbade her to make inflammatory remarks, or accusations about being left unattended. And he asked her to consider that

> God orders all things. Where there is no love, put love and you will draw out love.

In the cause for beatification, María de la Encarnación stated:

> These words have remained stamped on my soul to this day.

Fray Juan traveled to La Peñuela in Andalusia, the principal monastery of the province. From there he wrote to the father provincial, his friend from his Duruelo days, Antonio de Jesús, asking for instructions on where to wait for his departure to Mexico.

Father Antonio replied:

> Wherever it please Your Reverence to wait.

Fray Juan wrote:

> I am not here to do as I please or choose the roof over my head. Pray tell me where Your Reverence would like me to go and I will go there.

Knowing his friend, Father Antonio said he should stay where he was. La Peñuela was a remote monastery hidden away in the southern foothills of the Sierra Morena, the slopes of which are covered in rock roses, terebinths, wild figs, heather, madrones, kermes oaks and wild herbs.

The prior of this monastery, Fray Diego de la Concepción, said that Fray Juan, during his time there, ceaselessly gave thanks to God for being a simple friar once again, free of a prelate's responsibilities—indeed, free of any responsibility other than to his own soul.

His favorite place to pray was at the foot of a fountain encircled by trees. There he would remain until he heard the bell calling the community to the divine office. He would rise before dawn and go down to the garden. Kneeling beside an irrigation channel among the willows, he went through his morning prayers to the sound of running water. He considered it a luxury to sleep on some sprigs of rosemary woven together on a framework of vine shoots.

Then news came of the postponement of the expedition to Mexico. The reason for this was unknown. It gave María de la Encarnación, chief among the protestors, an opportunity to call for his reinstatement as prior of the Discalced monastery in Segovia. Fray Juan wrote to her in alarm.

"God in His mercy", he wrote,

> has given me leave to be free of all care but that of my own soul. And I assure you I am more at ease among rocks and trees than among people.

The tenacious prioress of Segovia was scheming with the influential Ana de Peñalosa to persuade the saint to change his mind when on September 27, 1591 Doña Ana received a letter.

"My lady," the saint wrote,

> I fear I have caught a chill. For the last week or so I have had a slight fever that comes on in the evening. My superiors have decided that I am in need of attention. Regrettably, this is not to be had in La Peñuela. Tomorrow I journey to Úbeda, where there is a good physician. As soon as I am well again, I shall return here. Your ladyship and Reverend Mother María de la Encarnación may do as you wish in your endeavors to restore me to the position of prior of Segovia. But it will not avail you, for I have prayed to God to let me die unencumbered by a prelate's responsibilities. And, God

willing, I shall return to La Peñuela as soon as I have the strength to set out on this last good journey.

On September 28, 1591, Fray Juan set off for Úbeda with a young lad. There was a doctor in Úbeda who was devoted to the Carmelite Order, attending the friars free of charge and even paying for medicines out of his own pocket. The saint's swollen leg made it impossible for him to walk, and he was on a gelding belonging to a man by the name of Juan de Cuellar who was from Úbeda. Although the leg had been swollen for several months, Fray Juan had said nothing about it. It was only when the prior found out that the saint had a fever and was suffering from chills that made him shiver that he ordered Fray Juan to Úbeda.

"It would appear that Your Reverence prefers giving orders to taking them", the prior remarked tartly when Fray Juan protested.

"If it is a question of obedience," he replied meekly, "I will go."

The road from La Peñuela to Úbeda wound its way through rolling hills covered with poplars, oleanders and tamarisks. Giving no sign of the pain his leg must have been causing him, Fray Juan was in high spirits, singing and praying by turns. The two travelers stopped at midday to rest.

Fray Juan told the lad to eat. He himself would not do so, adding that it had been several days since he had last been able to keep anything down.

"But", the lad protested, "I promised the prior to make sure Your Reverence ate something, whether you wanted to or not. Tell me what you would like and I will fetch it."

"In that case," the saint replied, "I'll have some asparagus if you can find any."

"Asparagus!" the lad exclaimed. "At this time of year? Is Your Reverence making fun of me?"

It was then late September. Yet, as they passed a vegetable plot by the roadside, they were both surprised to see some wild asparagus, or *sprew*, as it is sometimes known. Shaking his head and muttering something about a miracle, the lad picked the asparagus.

"Put a stone where the asparagus was", said the saint, "and leave these four *maravedíes* on it, for miracle or no, the owner is likely to feel robbed."

When they arrived, the story of the asparagus quickly spread through the monastery. Some of the friars said it was a miracle, as asparagus was out of season. Others said it was not and that in the shelter of the Guadalimar bridge asparagus could sometimes be found at that time of year. Fray Juan played the incident down and asked the cook to prepare it in case it worked like manna.

"So much for your miracle", he said when the asparagus made him vomit, like everything else he had eaten recently.

The doctor, Ambrosio de Villareal, examined the patient. He was not as concerned about the swollen leg as about the body as a whole. His diagnosis was erysipelas. In a reasonably healthy person, this is not serious. In a person whose health was as fragile as Fray Juan's, it was potentially life threatening. He also told the prior, Fray Francisco Crisóstomo, that the disease was contagious and that he should take precautions. This was unfortunate for Fray Juan. The prior, who had also been censured by Fray Juan for vainglory in the pulpit, ordered Fray Juan to be moved to the smallest and meanest cell in the monastery, on the pretext of the danger of contagion. In the refectory, he was made to sit at the end of the table, separate from the others, as if he had the plague.

But Fray Juan's humiliation was short-lived. The infection spread, and he was soon unable to go down to the refectory. His leg broke out in five sores in the shape of the

Cross, from which a musky, amber-colored pus oozed. The saint derived much comfort from these weeping sores. The largest, the one on his instep, was in the exact position of one of the stigmata. The pain these caused the saint made him deeply reverential. He was soon too weak to rise from the low wooden bench on which he lay.

To the horror of the friars nursing the saint, the doctor decided to lance the leg and scrape out the wounds. Fray Juan did not utter a sound during these terrible procedures. At last the doctor exclaimed, "For pity's sake, Father, why do you not cry out? My courage fails me at the thought that I am working on dead flesh."

"Of what would you have me complain", Fray Juan calmly replied, "when my condition is a blessing to me? Job had to clean his wounds with a potsherd, whereas I have fine cloths and many people tending me."

There was some truth in this. He was already being spoken about as a saint. And the quiet way he bore his painful condition meant that every single member of the community wanted to nurse him, with one exception—the prior, of whom his subordinate Alonso de la Madre de Dios said: "He was exceedingly severe and felt a special enmity toward those reputed to be saints." The prior took every opportunity to mortify Fray Juan. The saint's best nurse was a lay brother by the name of Fray Bernardo de la Virgen, whose great strength enabled him to pick up the patient and turn him without touching any of the numerous abscesses that now covered his whole body. The prior forbade Fray Bernardo to continue to nurse the saint because he disapproved of favoritism among his friars, a decision at which the lay brother wept.

"Why do you weep, Brother?" Fray Juan gently inquired. "Do you not see that this is what I want? It has always been my fervent hope that Our Lord would let me die unburdened by a prelate's responsibilities and with some small mortification or other to shorten my time in purgatory. And in my present condition I can think of no greater mortification than to forgo the gentle touch of your hands."

Fortunately he did not have to forgo it for long. Fray Bernardo de la Virgen wrote to Father Antonio de Jesús informing him of what was going on in Úbeda. The provincial immediately came to the monastery. He rebuked the prior and reinstated Fray Bernardo as chief nurse. By now it was mid-December. Fray Juan was in constant pain, his whole body one suppurating sore. He never lost consciousness, however. Shortly before his death, in an attempt to comfort him, Father Antonio said, "Be of good courage, Father and put your trust in God. Remember how hard we worked at the beginning of our Order?"

"Do not remind me, Father", Fray Juan replied. "Tell me rather of my sins."

Another time, when Fray Antonio was talking about the privations they had endured at the beginning of the Reform in Duruelo, Fray Juan said, "Did we not agree, Father, that we would not boast about that again?"

With what little strength remained to him, he protested when he discovered that his dressings, which were said to give off a sweet perfume, were not being thrown away but distributed among his devotees like relics.

"What is this madness?" he said to the doctor, who was the chief culprit in this trade. "Is what seeps from my wounds not infectious? Yet you allow it to be passed around."

"I not only allow it," the doctor replied, "I encourage it."

Fray Juan's stoicism had impressed the doctor so much that he had become his most devoted follower. "If this is the contagion of sainthood," he continued, "then I too want to be infected by it."

On December 11, the saint requested viaticum. According to the custom in all Discalced houses, he received this in the presence of the whole community. He took this opportunity to ask the prior's forgiveness for all the trouble he had caused him in his illness. He also asked his blessing for the journey that lay ahead. At this, Father Francisco Crisóstomo's resentment melted, and after giving his blessing, he left the cell in tears.

In his own deposition, the postulator in the cause for beatification, Father Alonso de la Madre de Dios, states:

> We thought he would die that day, for he was in a good state of readiness and had said many things of great beauty, so that there remained little for him to do in this world. But it was not to be until three days thence. He already knew as much, the Blessed Virgin having appeared to him in a vision eight days previously. We knew this because time and again when we thought he had died, so still and peaceful was he, he would open his eyes and say, "Blest be Our Lady for wanting me to depart on her day, Saturday."
>
> He no longer even had the strength to feel pain. Or if he did, he succeeded in hiding it. We were all with him on the Friday when sometime after nightfall he opened his eyes and entreated us most earnestly to go and rest and that when the time came he would call us. Some of us stayed with him. The next time he asked what hour it was, we told him it wanted but a half hour of midnight. Then his visage suffused with joy. And lifting his voice, he said:
>
> "At last the time draws near. You may call the others."
>
> When all were present he raised himself with the aid of a rope that hung from the ceiling, and said:
>
> "Let us recite the *De profundis*, for I yet have some strength in me."

We did so, and also the *Miserere*. Then he rested a little. When it was but a quarter of an hour to midnight or so, in an endeavor to help him die well, I reminded him that it was yet Friday and that if he could hold on until midnight, he would gain the indulgence of the Sabbatine privilege of the scapular of Our Lady of Mount Carmel. And then the Blessed Virgin would take him straight from purgatory. He thanked me quietly but assured me there was no need. At midnight the bells of the Church of San Salvador rang, and shortly thereafter those of the monastery.

"For what do the bells ring?" Fray Juan earnestly inquired.

I replied it was for matins. Then he joyously exclaimed:

"Glory be to God. In Heaven will I say them."

And, kissing the crucifix he always wore about his neck, he expired. His visage, which was naturally of a sallow hue, grew pale and translucent. And from that body so racked with sores came a scent as of roses.